Triptych

Also by Claude Simon:

The Battle of Pharsalus
Conducting Bodies
The Flanders Road
The Grass
Histoire
The Palace
The Wind

Triptych
Claude Simon

Translated from the
French by Helen R. Lane

A Richard Seaver Book
The Viking Press
New York

A Richard Seaver Book / The Viking Press
First published in 1976 by The Viking Press, Inc.
625 Madison Avenue, New York, N.Y. 10022
Published simultaneously in Canada by
The Macmillan Company of Canada Limited
Printed in U.S.A.

Library of Congress Cataloging in Publication Data
Simon, Claude.
    Triptych.
    "A Richard Seaver book."
    Translation of Triptyque.
    I. Title.
PZ3.S59435Tr   [PQ2637.I547]   843'.9'14   75–46560
ISBN 0–670–73136–6

Triptych

The postcard shows an esplanade bordered by a row of palm trees standing out against a sky of too bright a blue, at the edge of a sea of too bright a blue. A long cliff of blinding white façades, with rococo decorations, follows the curve of the bay in a gently-sweeping arc. Exotic shrubbery and clusters of cannas are planted between the palm trees, forming a bouquet in the foreground of the photograph. The canna flowers are tinted a garish red and orange. People in light-colored clothing are walking back and forth on the embankment that separates the esplanade from the beach. The inking of the various colors does not precisely coincide with the contours of each of the objects, so that as a consequence the harsh green of the palm trees overlaps the blue of the sky, or the mauve of a scarf or a parasol encroaches on the ocher of the ground or the cobalt of the sea. The postcard is lying on the corner of a kitchen table covered with yellow, red, and pink checkered oilcloth, nicked in several places by the blades of cleavers or knives that have slipped. The ragged edges of the nicks have lifted away, and one can see the chestnut-colored backing of the oilcloth. Not far from the postcard, the pink body of a skinned rabbit is stretched out on a porcelain platter with thick edges. Its bloody head is dangling over the end of the platter, touching the oilcloth. The kitchen door opens directly onto a courtyard covered with gravel which separates the house from another building parallel to it. One of the ends of the courtyard is closed off by a wrought-iron gate with double doors. The other end opens onto a plum orchard. One can hear, very close by, the sound of water pouring over the low wall of a millrace and streaming through the sluice. Farther in the distance, fainter, lower in pitch, the sound of a waterfall can also be heard. The orchard extends as far as the river, just before the bend it makes as it heads toward the little village. Just past the bend, the current is partially diverted into the millrace, which flows underneath the first arch of a stone bridge, the second arch of which, downstream from the low wall, spans the sparkling free water flowing rapidly between little islands with clumps of water willow and enormous pale bluish green leaves shaped like flaring funnels. Near the bridge stands the church, separated from the road by a little terrace with four old walnut trees on it. The huge waterfall is situated approximately half a mile upstream from the little village which consists of no more than thirty houses. Leaving this hamlet, the road continues on in the direction of a sawmill at the foot of the waterfall. Before reaching it, the road forms a fork, the left branch of which leads past a barn not far away and then continues on toward the top of the valley. The church steeple can be seen from the barn. One can also see the steeple, though not the barn, from the foot of the waterfall. From the top of the waterfall both the steeple and the roof of the barn are visible. The steeple is square, built of gray stone and topped by a roof in the form of a pyramid covered with flat tiles. The outer edges of the pyramid are protected by galvanized metal strips which have rusted to a soft reddish gold. The sound of the great waterfall echoes off the sharp slopes of the valley and the rock cliffs. Lying in the meadow at the top of the waterfall, one can see the stalks of wild grasses and umbels outlined against the sky, their stems stirring in the breeze from time to time, the wild grasses with their more supple stems curving slightly, the umbels swaying stiffly back and forth. Viewed from this angle, the umbels are taller than the church steeple. In fact, it is not possible to look at both the umbels and the steeple at the same time. If one fixes one's gaze on the umbels, the church steeple in the distance appears as a vague gray rectangle, stood vertically on edge, topped by an equally vague violet-colored triangle. At certain hours of the day, the sun's rays cast a bright glint on one or the other of the rusted metal strips. The stems of the umbels are covered with a delicate white fuzz, surrounding them with a luminous halo when viewed against the light. On the slender pedicels supporting the heads of the flowerlets, spreading outward like the ribs of an umbrella, the downy hairs stretch out, join, and intermingle, forming a sort of snowy haze. The barn built on the sloping meadow, with walls made of more or less disjointed vertical planks, stands on an outcropping of stone. Upstream, this layer of stone is scarcely visible along the surface of the ground. In certain places, earth slides or rains have caused the dirt to pile up at the base of the wall made of planks, against which clumps of weeds are growing. If one fixes one's gaze on the church steeple, the stems and the flowers of the umbels change in turn into vague forms that sway gently back and forth, describing acute triangles whose imprecise sides alternately intersect and move apart. At the foot of the waterfall stands a sawmill which drains off a portion of the current via a small millrace. The massive roof of the sawmill is of the same dark purplish color as the church steeple, and its outer edges are also protected by galvanized metal strips rusted to a soft reddish-gold color. There is a noticeable smell of freshly-cut planks and sawdust. Between the sawmill and the church, the river runs across land with no abrupt drops, and the transparent water flows at an even rate, neither slow nor fast, over the yellowish-brown bottom of tuff-stone and pebbles. The southern side of the barn is covered with bright-colored advertising posters, one atop the other, the oldest of them torn and faded by exposure to the elements, with corners that have come unglued, the most recent of them a large-sized poster showing a circus ring where an animal tamer shod in shiny boots and armed with a whip is putting his trained wild beasts through one of their tricks. The poster is bordered by a yellow band spangled with red stars. Due to the alternate effects of humidity and heat, the planks forming the wall of the barn have become warped, swelling or contracting, so that a number of cracks have appeared in the posters pasted over them.

One of these cracks is wider than the others, however, and would seem to have been deliberately enlarged. At the foot of the waterfall a hollow has been formed, in the shape of an approximately circular basin, the bottom of which is invisible. On the edges of this basin the extremely clear water allows one to glimpse the ocher riverbed of tuff-stone. As the depth of the water increases, it first grows greener, and then becomes the color of laundry bluing, darkening by degrees, becoming almost black at the center of the basin. It takes a moment for the eye glued to the crack that has been enlarged to grow accustomed to the semidarkness within the barn and be able to make out various objects inside. The woods covering the slopes of the valley are bordered with coppices of hazelnut trees and hornbeam. The boundary of the woods winds up along the sloping meadows, forming curves, gulfs, and capes, one of which nearly touches the back side of the barn. Detached like an island from the leading edge of the forest, a dense thicket of hazelnut trees runs along parallel to the wall covered with posters for a distance of several yards. An old-model motorcycle is lying at the foot of the wall, hidden by the low branches with round, crinkly leaves which the slight breeze stirs from time to time. The mudguards, the pedals, the exhaust pipe, and even the gas tank, painted in black with metal strips that once were gold-colored, are covered, on those parts not subject to any sort of friction, with a layer of yellowish dust that has turned dark brown in the places where it has been spattered with oil and has formed a sort of greasy sludge on the chain sprocket. From the place where the barn stands, one can hear distinctly the powerful, continuous roar of the waterfall echoing off · the cliffs of gray rocks peeking out here and there among the dense foliage of the woods on the steep slopes of the valley which these rock faces surmount in certain spots, being themselves surmounted by clumps of scrubwood whose roots plunge downward through cracks in the rock and whose scraggly trunks twist upward against the sky, in which clouds drift calmly by, their sinuous or lacy contours endlessly changing shape, tracing blisters, gulfs, and capes which bulge out, form hollows, and disintegrate. If one fixes one's gaze on the clouds, it seems as though the cliffs are slowly tipping forward in a single block, dragging along with them their crown of vegetation, the wooded slopes, and the earth that has fallen at their feet, as though one entire side of the valley were about to tumble down and bury beneath a chaos of rocks and uprooted trees the little village, the river, and the church steeple whose galvanized metal strips shimmer above the light-colored foliage of the huge walnut trees. The sounds of the church bell tolling out the quarter-hours, the half-hours, and the hours also seem to echo off the rock cliffs and remain suspended in the calm air for a long time, continuing to reverberate, imponderable and metallic. One corner of the large circus poster that has come unglued hangs down, folded halfway back on itself. The same slight puffs of breeze that carry the sound of the bronze bell and stir the leaves of the hazelnut trees raise this corner and then allow it to fall back again. The planks of the barn wall, roughly coated with pitch, are of a dark brown color streaked with the light, grayish veins formed by the grain of the wood, standing out in slight relief. Between these veins the wood has a sort of plushy texture, somewhat like that of blotting paper, which can easily be scratched by a fingernail. The veins of the wood, all running in the same direction, form wavy lines like tresses of hair or the waters of a river, at times drawing farther apart from each other and then drawing closer together and touching to form a knot, like an island in a stream or an eye. Beyond the basin at the foot of the waterfall the course of the river bordered with bushes and trees describes two successive curves in opposite directions between the meadows, forming an S, and then skirts the village before running parallel to the wall of the church once again and passing under the bridge. The heads and torsos of the two boys lying flat on their bellies on the parapet of the bridge are reflected on the calm surface of the millrace. They are silhouetted in dark ocher against the reflection of the sky, cut off just a little below the shoulders by the straight line of the parapet. Inside the outline of the two silhouettes one can see the bottom of the river, the pebbles covered with yellowish moss, yellowish undulating algae, and a rusty barrel-hoop as well. The white clouds drift slowly around the two heads and the two torsos, blurring their contours. The lower edge of the large circus poster stops an inch or so above the stone foundation of the barn, leaving bare the bottom of the plank wall where the once-fresh pitch, slipping down beneath its own weight, has accumulated in thick, almost black layers. As it has dried, it has crazed and become covered with a network of fine cracks. The sloping meadow is planted with a mixture of clover and alfalfa. The clumps of weeds form a sort of frieze against the dark background of the tarred planks. The sharp stems are narrow and pointed, some of them jutting up stiffly, like sabers or yataghans, and some of them broken in two, with the point hanging downward, or else twisted back upon themselves. They have a shallow fold running down the length of them. One of the faces of the tiny dihedron has more of a bluish tinge than the other. The alfalfa leaves are oval, grouped in clusters. The flowers are purple. The aid of a knife has no doubt been necessary in order to dig into the layer upon layer of superimposed posters and enlarge the widest of the cracks made by the wood as it warped. The ocher circus ring has come unglued and rolled back on itself on one edge, baring the preceding poster. In the narrow triangle thus revealed, one can see a brick wall against which two silhouettes are locked in embrace. The light-colored mortar between the bricks in the wall, shown in perspective, runs off toward the left in converging lines. Above the wall, in the upper portion of the narrow triangle now visible, one can see the top of a factory chimney, also made of bricks, rising in a sky full of black clouds and smoke. The eye, blind at first, begins little by little to make out moving forms, white flesh sharply outlined against the darkness, in the dim shadow inside the barn. The two sides of the narrow slit severely limit the field of vision on the right and on the left. Beyond the rusted barrel-hoop, shards of pottery, pieces of roof tile, and a broken pitcher are mingled with the stones covering the river bottom. Certain of these bits of debris thrown down from the top of the bridge have been there for so long a time that they are covered with the same layer of impalpable ocher moss that covers the pebbles. Only the most recent debris (the pitcher, a blue enameled saucepan pierced by a hole with black edges) has retained its original color. It takes considerable time to make out the trout that is managing to remain in the same spot, despite the force of the current, by virtue of faint undulations of its black and ocher body among the flattened algae, which are also ocher and black, and also undulating in the same manner. Moreover, it is visible only in the zone of shadow cast by the parapet of the bridge and the contours of the two silhouettes, beyond and around which the reflection of the sky and the blindingly bright clouds prevent one from making out the bottom of the river. One of the boys stretches out his arm, one finger pointing in the direction of the trout, and the reflection of his torso moves closer to that of the other boy. Although neither one of them has spoken, the trout darts to the right with a rapid flick of its tail and slips through the mouth of the pitcher lying on its side. Before it disappears, the boys manage to catch a glimpse of its gleaming light-colored underbelly. When the man's pelvis moves backward, one glimpses for the fraction of a second his gleaming cylindrical member partly emerging from the thick black tuft of hair be-tween his bent thighs, which look faintly blue, like skim milk, and phosphorescent in the yellowish half-light of the barn. One of the boys warns the other in a whisper not to move and it will soon come out again. The white butterflies chase after each other, fluttering back and forth, their paths crossing, suddenly sinking in the air and then rising again above the clumps of water willows and broad leaves bathed in the shimmering light reflected from the rapid, free-flowing, shallow water that par-tially bares the bed of scaly white pebbles on which the dried moss is the yellowish color of tow. Other objects thrown down from the bridge or swept along by the winter floodwaters appear here and there: a man's high-top shoe of wrinkled, shriveled leather, with the vamp gaping open; a kettle; tin cans. Dead branches, bare and white, have been caught in, enmeshed in the sluice or their progress downstream arrested by the clumps of water willows. The sound of the jet of the fountain in front of the church can be clearly distinguished from that of the water roiling at the foot of the little dam. The fountain consists of a rectangular stone trough, resembling a sarcophagus, with a notch hacked out of one of its edges, through which the over-flow runs out in thin films that slide down the vertical face. Beneath the shade of the huge walnut trees, the surface of the water in the fountain is almost black, as though varnished, cease-lessly traversed by concentric wrinkles that continually grow larger and larger and die away little by little as they travel farther outward from the point where the jet of water falls and where the reflections of the leaves of the walnut trees and frag-ments of sky come together and draw apart in a perpetual quivering motion. The inner walls of the basin are covered with long strings of green moss, bits of which drift out horizontally, stirred from time to time by the faint motions of the water that feeds the jet. Its vegetative luxuriance contrasts with the smooth surface of the stone. The thick black fleece in which the shining member continues its motion back and forth contrasts with the smooth whiteness of the buttocks and the thighs. The base of the stiff, muscular member disappears amid a thicket of hairs with a reddish cast. The man's thighs, cut off just a little above the knee by the torn edge of the slit opened up in the poster, are covered with dark hairs that also have a reddish cast, and that become sparser toward the top of his thighs and disappear alto-gether on his buttocks. If one wets one's hand in the fountain, it seems as though it has been gripped by an icy glove that ends abruptly at the wrist. Beneath one's fingers the long green tufts of moss have a soft and velvety feel. If one pulls one of them out, it clings to one's fingers and feels slightly sticky, like wet cotton. One of the boys nudges the other with his elbow. Moving rapidly in an oblique line across the bed of the river, a second trout emerges from underneath the bridge, hesitates, turns back toward the left, lazily allows itself to be carried backward by the current, darts quickly off again, and finally lies motionless in the water, approximately in the middle of the riverbed, where it manages to remain in the same spot by virtue of faint undulations of its tail. Five or six cows being driven along by a tow-headed lad, whose hair has been cropped off in a ragged line across the nape of his neck with a pair of scissors, move slowly across the bridge, their bony haunches swaying stiffly from side to side. Their hides are russet with large white spots. One of them stops and turns its head sideways toward the parapet over which the two boys are still leaning. Indifferent to the cries of the lad poking its hindquarters with his stick, it raises its tail and releases a greenish, pasty flow of dung that spreads out on the ground between its hoofs with a splatting sound. A few spatters land on its hoofs and a few sticky trickles cling to its hocks. The lad goes over to the parapet and leans over it to see what the two older boys are watching. Passing abruptly from its lazy state of immobility to motion, the trout darts away like an arrow and disappears upstream in the zone hidden from view by the blinding reflection of the sky, allowing the trace of its rigid, elongated form, propelled solely by the rapid wrigglings of its tail, to persist on the retina. One of the boys raises his torso and hurls insults at the lad. The lad shrugs his shoulders and says You didn't think you were going to catch it here, did you?, then starts running after his cows, his feet weighted down by his wooden shoes that knock together. With raucous cries, in the voice of a teamster that is altogether out of proportion to his size, he prods with the sharp end of his stick the haunches of the cow that is loitering, thus causing it to break into an awkward trot. As it draws away, one can see its pink udders swinging ponderously, like church bells, appearing alternately on one side and the other of its ill-shapen hocks covered with a layer of dark brown, almost black, dung with cracks in it. Having rejoined the others, it falls in step with them. On the bridge, the fresh cow-pie forms a round pile, as wide as a platter, the soft substance rising up in concentric layers with rounded edges, one atop the other. Two other piles of diminishing size are followed by the trail of liquid spatters that the cow has left behind as it set off again. A cloud of minuscule gnats circles round and round above the turds, together with a butterfly with red and black wings. The butterfly finally flutters off and alights on an umbel growing in a clump with several others at the base of one of the ends of the parapet, and perches there motionless. With its wings folded tightly together, it is no thicker than a sheet of paper, and dull brown in color. The couple locked in embrace against the brick wall are apparently motionless. After a moment one perceives, however, that the right arm of the man who is holding his companion with her back to the wall is making faint motions back and forth, imparted to it by the invisible hand slipped underneath the girl's raised skirt, thus revealing a little patch of white skin above her stocking. The man is dressed in a black suit. He occasionally moves a short distance away, and one then catches a glimpse of his white shirt front gleaming in the shadow and the black bow tie fastened around the collar. The corner of the circus poster that has come unglued affords a glimpse, at his feet and behind him, of paving stones glistening in the rain. From the road that leads to the sawmill one is not able to see the motorcycle. In the meadow, however, the wheels have left long tracks leading to the clump of hazelnut trees near the barn. Along the entire length of these tracks, the grass has been irregularly trampled down by the feet of the man walking alongside the motorcycle as he pushed it. One can smell the odor of crushed grass. Having been momentarily flattened beneath the wheels of the motorcycle or the man's shoes, the blades of grass are beginning to straighten up again. On the other hand, at the foot of the clump of hazelnut trees whose low branches hide the motorcycle, the alfalfa and the clover are crushed beneath the weight of the heavy machine. A purple alfalfa flower, already wilted, is hanging downward, its stem broken across the middle, forming an acute angle. An umbel, still intact, is standing in the empty space between the front wheel and the frame of the motorcycle. Behind the saddle is a narrow seat, shaped like a roof tile, covered in black moleskin. There is no dust on the moleskin of the seat, nor on the saddle, except in the holes of the stitching around their edges. Clinging here and there to the saddlebags hanging down on each side of the seat, just behind it, is a layer of dust, which one can see because of the position of the machine, lying on its side. The dust, darkened by grease and oily exhaust fumes, is the same ocher color as the moss that covers the stones at the bottom of the river or the discarded objects thrown down into it from the bridge. The dried mud on the black moleskin is a pale gray color. A damp coolness is beginning to rise from the meadows. The slit in the torn poster allows one to see only the mid-section of the two bodies, the right-hand edge cutting off the view of everything except the woman's hip, her buttock, her thigh bent back, her two feet that she has wrapped around the man's back, and the man's hairy thighs, his pants pulled down in accordion folds that hide his knees from view, and his legs cut off just below by the left-hand edge of the slit. The back-and-forth motion of the man's buttocks becomes more and more rapid and greater and greater in amplitude. The purplish glans appears from time to time, only to immediately disappear again. It is necessary to climb higher in the woods to reach the young fir plantation. Amid the thin pinkish trunks, planted close together, one finds oneself in the torpid semidarkness of a church or a sanctuary, and the silence seems deeper still. No weed, no plant grows on the thick rust-colored carpet of pine needles that covers the ground and muffles the sound of footsteps. There are edible mushrooms growing in little patches here, not far from the bottoms of the trees. They have white stems and rounded caps of a purplish-brown color. The fir plantation makes a dark green, almost black, spot among the leaves of the beech and ash trees. The light spot, phosphorescent in the darkness, formed by the girl's thigh entwined around her companion, has grown larger. Standing on her other leg and leaning her back against the brick wall, she has brought her thigh up against his belly and with her hand is guiding inside her the stiff member of the man, the skin of which appears all the more white, it too almost phosphorescent, because of the fact that it emerges, pointing straight upward, from the black pants of what appears to be evening dress, or in any event a dress suit. The man has bent his knees slightly, the better to penetrate the girl. He appears to be tottering and might perhaps fall down if she were not holding him up. The girl's stockings are of a coppery chestnut color, stopping at mid-thigh. The patch of flesh that is thus bared (the two faces are now invisible, that of the girl hidden by the head of the man, who is kissing her on the neck, his head being three-quarters buried in her copper-colored locks—the poster-painter having used the same color for the stockings and the hair) constitutes the only light note in the composition, otherwise made up entirely of dark colors (black, the purplish red of the bricks of the wall, smoke or dark clouds), revealed by the panel of the circus poster that has come unglued. A huge clown's head completely fills another poster (this one in the form of a vertical rectangle) pasted edge-to-edge against the one showing the wild-animal tamer in the shiny boots above whose head tigers are leaping. The copper-colored stocking covers the bent, raised knee, the calf, and the foot shod in a high-heeled pump which the couple's movements cause to sway back and forth at the level of the man's thigh. A ladybug with a red carapace dotted with symmetrically arranged black spots is slowly making its way across the round ball with an uneven surface formed by the cluster of white flowerlets of the umbel. With its delicate antennae spread apart in a V, it cautiously explores the minuscule corollas. Suddenly it raises its wing cases, causing its delicate transparent black wings to become visible, whereupon it unfolds them and takes flight. A middle-aged, quite fat man, dressed in black, is standing on the red carpet of a room illuminated by a harsh light. With his feet together, he turns his head to one side, his face thus directly confronting the spectator, as though he were trying to hear some sound or some voice through the panel of the door, the handle of which he is holding in one hand. Contrasting sharply with the light-colored wall and the red carpet, the dark-colored suit absorbs the light, the whole (the folds of the cloth, the edges of the jacket or the vest) dissolving into a patch with soft, sinuous contours, like those of an ink spot or one of those silhouettes of birds standing motionless on one leg, hunched up inside their plumage, this black patch being surmounted by a pinkish head, with purple blotches on the face and soft skin that hangs down in folds beneath its own weight, accentuating, despite its flabbiness, the bony ridges of the cheekbones. The torso is bent slightly forward, projecting toward the door the face with half-closed eyes, a short nose, and thick lips, which bears a perplexed, attentive, and pathetic expression. The forearm, at the end of which the hand is grasping the door handle, juts out horizontally from the black patch at the level of the belly, like the arm of a gibbet. After a moment, either out of indecision, or because the door is locked from the other side, the hand lets go of the door handle and falls back along the body, which remains in the same position, the torso still bending forward, the face in wine-colored tones sharply outlined in the light and etched with black shadows. On the pathetic face of the clown outlined by the pallid beam of the spotlight, sweat thins out the white grease paint that gleams on his temples and cheeks. In the background, in the shadow, one can vaguely make out the torsos of the spectators sitting next to each other on the circular tiers of benches that form a sort of huge funnel. The wet sawdust of the circus ring is the same color as the dark chestnut-brown stockings and hair of the girl leaning against the brick wall. Although still wobbling on his feet, her companion begins to swing his pelvis in a back-and-forth motion. The edge of the circus ring, consisting of whitewashed boxes, at the base of which the horses' hoofs have left brown marks, forms a perfect circle. The boy's hand traces on the page of the notebook a triangle, the circle it describes, and a tangent to this circle parallel to one of the sides of the triangle. Next to each of the angles of the triangle he inscribes the letters A, B, and C. Then he extends the sides BA and BC, which intersect the tangent parallel to the side AC at two points, A' and C'. Drawn freehand, the circle is slightly flattened, like the outline of an apple, and the various straight lines are slightly wavy. The figure is nonetheless sufficiently precise to allow the boy to reflect on the problem posed, the text of which he reads a second time on the page of the open textbook lying on the table to the right of the notebook: "Given the degree of the angle ABC, prove: 1) that the relationship of the surfaces of the triangles ABC and A'B'C' is proportional to . . ." Penetrating through the open window, the sun projects in the room a parallelogram of light, one of whose sides cuts diagonally across the upper right-hand corner of the page of the notebook where the figure is drawn, forming a dazzlingly bright equilateral triangle. The boy sees the grassy plum orchard, framed by the window, sloping gently down to the river. A tiny silhouette of a woman stooping over, or rather, bent almost double, is outlined in black against the bright light-colored background made up of acid greens gleaming in the sunlight. The woman is wearing a dark yellow straw hat whose broad brim is tied back at each side of her head by a dark scarf running over the crown and knotted underneath her chin. Unkempt gray locks of hair have escaped the confines of this headgear and fallen down over her forehead. All the lower part of her face and her chin jut out like those of certain species of monkeys or dogs. Underneath the floppy skirt flapping about her calves one can see her thin ankles, clad in loose-fitting, twisted black stockings. Her feet are shod in men's heavy high-top shoes without laces. The sleeves of her black work-smock are rolled up, baring her bony forearms covered with yellowish skin. From the end of one of them, held out horizontally at a right angle to the vertical axis of her body, there dangles a rabbit with pearl-gray fur being held by the ears, at times absolutely motionless and at times jerking its haunches helplessly. Now and then one catches a glimpse of the gleaming blade of a knife being held in the gnarled yellow fingers of her other hand. The girl lying in the hay accompanies with jerks of her hips the rhythmic back-and-forth motion of the buttocks of the man, whose glistening member gleams for a moment each time that it is withdrawn, and then immediately disappears again up to the balls between the bushy bright black hairs, as curly as astrakhan. The couple are in an area of half-shadow beyond the luminous cone of light projected at the entrance to the narrow passage between the brick walls by an arc light attached to the top of a metal pole with crisscrossing girders. Little drops of fine mist rain down in a glistening powder in the upper part of the cone where the light condenses. In the background one can see here and there, piercing the darkness of the night, several more of these cones, the intensity of whose light decreases as they widen out at the bottom. The height of the pylons at the top of which these arc lights are placed, their distribution throughout a vast area, lead one to presume that beyond the brick wall they illuminate some warehouse, the inner courtyards of a factory, or perhaps one of those huge dark spaces with a multitude of parallel streaks, the rails of a switchyard, glistening in the rain. From time to time there come from this area the echoes of coupling buffers and metal colliding. In the intervals filled by the silence that somehow seems even more profound amid the darkness and the feeble hissing of the fine drizzle, one can hear the intermingled panting breaths of the couple locked in embrace. The girl's chestnut-colored hair has taken on a deep brown tint and is beginning to hang down in damp hanks over her cheeks. From time to time, as her companion thrusts harder, the back of her head knocks against the rough bricks of the wall. These latter are not of a uniform color. Fired in a different way or made of different types of clay, they range from dark copper to blue-gray, passing through a whole series of different more or less deep shades of browns and purples. They are held together by a yellowish mortar, dirtied by the smoke and also rough in texture. Below the knee sheathed in silk and still raised high in the air, the leg swings back and forth in time with the man's thrusts. The body of the rabbit sways back and forth in time with the footsteps of the old woman walking with a jerky stride toward one of the plum trees with a low fork in its trunk. The breeze intermittently bends the branch of an invisible tree growing near the wall, and the intermingled shadows of the leaves sweep from the upper corner of the page of the notebook the triangle of sunlight whose oblique side now slightly overlaps the lower right angle of the triangle A'B'C'. Moving across each other, intersecting each other, the long oval shadows allow to pass through them only feeble rays of sunlight which trace on the table and the white page triangles, squares, or rectangles with curving concave sides, gliding about, dissolving, drawing closer together, moving farther apart, re-forming, all very rapidly, until the branch moves again, the intermingled patches of light and shadow thus borne upward suddenly disappearing, leaving the blindingly bright square of sunlight empty once again. With the point of his pen twirling rapidly round and round in the same spot, the boy marks the center of the circumscribed circle and traces alongside it the letter O. He then projects from it two straight lines ending at angles A and C of the initial triangle and writes below the figure the equation:

$$\widehat{ABC} = \frac{\widehat{AOC}}{2}$$

He contemplates his work for a moment, frowning, turning the end of the fountain pen round and round between his lips. When he raises his eyes again, his gaze glides past the paper and in the space enclosed by the window frame he sees once again the sunlit orchard where the thin black form with its arms upraised is now tying the rabbit by its paws, head downward, to the low branch of a plum tree. From time to time the animal continues to jerk its haunches or twist its body to one side, and then it gives up and the inert body continues to sway back and forth. Laying his pen down, the boy unbuttons one of the breast pockets of his shirt and removes from it two strips of movie film of unequal length, one of them consisting of six frames, the other of only four, bordered by little holes along the sides. Holding one of the strips up to the light, he looks through one of the little transparent rectangles, showing two persons sitting behind a low table on which there are drinking glasses and an ashtray. The frame as a whole is dark, like the inside of a bar, for example, and only the two faces, the shirt fronts, the hands, and the porcelain ashtray form light patches. Between the two persons, the boy can see the black silhouette of the old woman moving beneath the plum tree. The light patches of the faces, the shirt fronts, and the hands become vague and fuzzy, seemingly suspended in front of the luminous background of the orchard, where the various hues of green seen through the dark film are reduced to a uniform range of dull green tones differing only in intensity. The rabbit is now firmly attached by its hind paws to the low branch of the plum tree. The old woman with the bent back stoops over still farther and picks up a little stick lying at the foot of the tree. The sunlight casts a yellow glow through the front edge of the brim of the straw hat tied back on each side by the scarf knotted under her chin. This front edge, which forms a sort of visor, is ragged. From a little notch in it there hangs in a short broken line a bit of straw, of a golden-yellow color against the light. The rabbit's haunches continue to wriggle now and again, though more and more feebly, as if it had lost heart. The woman raises the stick that she is holding in the hand of her outstretched arm and lowers it, giving the rabbit a sharp blow on the neck. Doubtless the blow was badly aimed, for the rabbit's body suddenly gives a jerk and twists about in a circle. Arresting its movements back and forth with her other hand, the old woman strikes a second blow. The rabbit's body becomes inert and the periods of oscillation caused by the blow grow shorter and shorter. The old woman strikes a third blow with her stick in the same spot, and then throws the stick down at the foot of the tree. Opening the drawer of his table, the boy takes out a magnifying glass, and raising the strip of film in his left hand again, begins examining the little images in detail. He is thus able to make out more clearly the faces of the two protagonists. One of them is a middle-aged, quite fat man, with thick lips, a rather flat nose, and a high forehead left bare by his hair combed straight back. He is dressed in a dark suit with a buttoned vest. With his torso supported on either side by his arms, his hands resting flat on the banquette, his gaze reduced to a slit between his half-closed eyelids, his face bearing an anxious, perplexed expression, he is apparently having some difficulty hearing, as though the words were coming to him through a door or the obstacle of a foreign language, what is being said by the other person, who has a bird's profile, an aquiline nose, bushy eyebrows, and thin lips. This second man is dressed in a light-colored suit without a vest, his unbuttoned jacket revealing the front of a pale blue shirt and a tie held in place by a metal clip. He is sitting there in a nonchalant and offhand manner, with one of his arms resting on the back of the banquette. Most probably, he is emphasizing his words with rapid gestures, for his other arm, at the end of which his hand with the palm upturned and the fingers spread apart keeps circling round and round, leaves a murky trace on the film, whereas the movement of his forearm, from the elbow down, produces a light-colored angle streaked with concentric curves. Armed once again with her knife, with only the point of the blade jutting out past her clenched fist, the old woman with the head like a dog's gouges out one of the rabbit's eyes with a brusque movement of her wrist. At the same time, her left hand holds a bowl with a chipped edge underneath the emptied eye socket. The drops of blood, falling slowly at first and then faster and faster, splash into the bowl, leaving large bright-red spots on the concave inner surface of yellowish-gray porcelain crazed with a network of fine cracks. Sliding down toward the bottom, the drops of blood elongate and form ovals, fall closer and closer together, and soon a vertical thread links the empty eye socket to the bowl, where the level of blood caught in it rises little by little. Impregnating the porous bricks, the fine mist makes the colors of them more vivid, purple, steel blue, plum, red-orange. Somewhere beyond the wall one can hear an invisible locomotive shunting back and forth, and puffs of gray smoke, which also looks as though it were wet, rise and drift apart in the light of the arc lamps. The couple is hidden behind the protrusion formed by beer or lemonade cases with slatted sides painted in pastel colors (pink, yellow, or pale blue), piled up against the wall. At the entrance to the blind alley, a large old-model motorcycle is parked on its stand. The rain slowly dissolves the yellowish mud dirtying the forks, the crankcase, the spokes of the wheels, the bottom of the bulging gas tank, and the black moleskin bags behind the seat, but clings in shining little drops to the parts of the mechanism (the chain sprocket, the wheel axles, certain portions of the forks) where the oil and grease have caused the dust to accumulate in sticky dark brown patches. With her head thrown back and her face wet with rain, the girl repeats at regular intervals Yes yes oh yes. The man presses his head with the curly tow-colored hair against her freely-offered white neck. From one image to the other the position of the limbs and the heads of the two persons varies only slightly, save for that of the arm of the man in the light suit, which he continues to wave up and down. An unforeseen event (a third person suddenly entering the bar perhaps, or perhaps only the bartender coming over unexpectedly to take their orders for another round of drinks) must have occurred, however, for in the last two images one can see the head of the bird-man pivot from right to left so rapidly (either because he has been taken by surprise, or because all his movements—like those of his arm a short while before—are characterized by the same brusqueness) that two profiles of it are visible at the same time, turned in opposite directions and linked by a light-colored line intersected horizontally by dark streaks at the level of his eyes and mouth, as though the space between the two profiles had been swept with the stroke of a brush whose bristles were unevenly coated with paint. Hearing a noise, the boy gives a start, quickly slips the magnifying glass in the pocket of his short pants and the two fragments of film between the pages of the notebook, leaning over it again with his fountain pen in his hand. The door, which is behind his back, opens then and a little girl's voice asks a question which he answers in a surly tone of voice without turning around. The door then closes again. The boy remains in the same position for a moment, contemplating the geometric figure drawn on the white page where the square of sunlight has grown still larger. After a moment he draws a small arc of a circle going from one of the sides of the angle $\widehat{ABC}$ to the other, not far from its apex, whereupon he repeats the operation for the angle $\widehat{AOC}$, this time, however, drawing another small curving line directly alongside the other to make it darker. This done, he removes the two strips of film from the pages of the notebook and sticks them back in his shirt pocket. The folding panel of a transom for ventilation suddenly swings open with a bang at the second-floor level in the high bare wall, also made of bricks, bordering the alleyway on the side opposite the one against which the two lovers are leaning. A nearly horizontal beam of yellow light comes streaking out of it, piercing the darkness and gradually growing dimmer, though it clearly reveals near the opening of the transom the oblique, silvery, crisscrossing streaks of rain, now falling in faster, heavier drops. From the transom there also comes a sputtering noise, louder than that of the monotonous rain that is wetting, as far as the eye can see, the paving stones, the rails, the chimneys, the sheds, the block after block of dark red houses, the slag heaps, the little gardens, the warehouses, the trees of the squares or wooded areas, the whole of the landscape that is at once urban, industrial, and rural stretching out in the rain-soaked shadows pierced here and there by rare beams of light. Disturbed by the jerky movements of the couple, the beige coat that the girl has simply thrown over her shoulders before going out of doors has slid down and one of its ends is dragging in the mud, the top of it held up only by the pressure of her back against the wall and baring the silk blouse that the rain is plastering against the contours of her body. Drowning out the panting breaths of the man and the woman, a thundering voice with metallic resonances, with inflections at once emphatic and overbearing, mingles with the crackling sound of the film projector installed in the booth ventilated by the transom. In the blindingly bright beam of the spotlight the clown with his face smeared with garish makeup is entering the circus ring with a grotesque duck-waddle. From his mouth surrounded by a wide ring of red grease paint there escape raucous, somewhat frightening sounds, as though amplified by a loudspeaker, closely resembling those inarticulate wild cries that from time to time ring out in zoos, emitted by some exotic species of bird or ill-tempered monkeys in their cages. A quiver of laughter mingled with a vague feeling of apprehension runs along the surface of the funnel where the spectators are sitting in tiers in the darkness. Impalpable little motes of dust whirl about, gleaming in the pale beam of the spotlight. Dust and blue spirals of smoke, curling and uncurling, are suspended in the shaft of light coming from the projection booth and passing from this latter to the screen above the heads of the spectators. Moving streaks whose intensity ranges from white to black sweep over the luminous shaft of light, corresponding to the movements of the lights and shadows on the screen. In the brief intervals of silence between the thundering voice of the off-screen commentator and the bursts of music serving as an accompaniment, one again perceives, like a permanent back-ground sound, the regular crackling noise of the projector. With each of the movements within the shaft of light, rigid silken patches, either luminous or dark, correspond on the screen to the modifications of the image projected. White façades with pretentious decorations slowly file past from right to left, si-multaneously animated by two motions, that is to say, jerking rapidly up and down, as a consequence, doubtless, of the worn-out condition of the projector, this first movement, whose periods are short, being superimposed upon another which is also in a vertical plane, this latter movement being a conse-quence of the fact that the film has been shot from a boat, probably a motor launch, moving along the shore, rising and falling with the waves. The series of façades is sometimes hidden for a brief moment from the spectators' view (the screen suddenly lighting up then, entirely occupied by a white surface decorated with a large numeral) when the sail of a boat inter-poses itself between the launch and the shoreline, the successive rows of spectators' faces suddenly emerging from the darkness and then more or less rapidly disappearing back into it (depend-ing on whether the sailboat is navigating in the opposite di-rection from the launch or the same direction) as the billowing white surface disappears in turn on the left, revealing the pre-tentious buildings that rise and fall as though the dazzling façades, the tall palms, the sea wall, the beach with its smooth pebbles, its cabanas, and its bathers were being borne along by some immense raft riding on the waves and being gently tossed about. Some of the bathers lying stretched out on the beach or children standing at the water's edge wave their arms and make gestures in the direction of the spectators, or rather, in the direction of the motor launch on which they have doubt-less spied the movie camera and the film crew. The orchestra providing the accompaniment, in which violins predominate, plays a sloppily sentimental number that reminds one of the pieces played in cafés or casinos by fusty old-fashioned orchestras perched on podiums draped in red velvet and surrounded by green potted plants. The variations in intensity of the sound as the volume of the musical accompaniment is amplified or muffled in order to allow the voice of the commentator to be heard accentuate still further the vague feeling of nausea brought on by the rising or falling movement of the row of façades and the sea wall whose horizontal glide slows down, the camera which has been passing in review the succession of luxury hotels now remaining pointed at a much larger construction which thus occupies the entire screen, its various details (balconies, entablatures, cornices, domes, columns, capitals, corbels, clusters of foreign flags floating at the windows) each moving slowly in relation to the others, as though the enormous baroque edifice were mounted on a revolving platform and majestically pivoting, like those masterpieces of the art of pastry-making pretentiously displayed in the window of a confectioner's shop, the stentorian voice of the commentator becoming at the same time more pompous as the words that he articulates (centuries-old, sumptuous, kings, palace, luxury, splendid) seem also to turn slowly round and round, as though they were filing past in blazing letters on one of those illuminated signs running around the corners of newspaper buildings or advertising agencies, trailing behind them on one's bedazzled retina clusters of luminous aigrettes. The blindingly white monumental façade is framed by two massive towers, set slightly forward and surmounted by ponderous pink cupolas equipped with lightning rods. The cupolas have a vaguely phallic appearance, reminiscent of the caps of certain mushrooms. The tops of the tall palm trees sway back and forth at the level of the third-story windows. The pink-tinged naked body of a woman is sprawled out on a rumpled bed, absolutely motionless except for the left hand and arm, which stir languidly from time to time, as though to chase away a fly or a troubling thought or some slight cause for concern. A few drops of sweat form at the armpits and in the folds of the groin veiled by a downy tuft of blond hairs.

Her right arm is bent beneath her head, her legs are spread apart with the knees flexed, one of them resting flat on the sheet, the other in a vertical plane, with the heel nearly touching her buttock. The damp, wrinkled sheet bares a portion of the mattress, of a yellowish-brown color with narrow parallel stripes in groups of three. The walls are bare, like those of hotel rooms decorated with nothing but a few engravings, which the eye of the viewer registers only as dark rectangular patches standing out against the monotone background. The body appears to be disarticulated, inanimate, as though it had landed flat on the bed after a fall from a height of several stories. Yet the chest, the breasts with a light green shadow falling across them, and the belly rise and fall regularly with each breath. The movements of the left hand and arm, as though chasing away flies, vague and seemingly incomplete, resemble those sometimes made by a person in his sleep. The eyes, however, are wide open in the face with delicate features that is just a bit too pink, the skin ruined by the excessive use of makeup and the flabby flesh forming a contrast with the color and contours of the body, which are still beautiful, with pale-tipped breasts that have sagged only very slightly. The image in the mirror on the half-open door of a standing wardrobe reflects a portion of the body with its legs parted: the feet with painted toenails in the foreground, the foot of the leg resting on its side revealing its wrinkled sole, of a light ocher color, and its apricot-colored heel. The thighs cast pearly reflections, and they too have a green shadow across them. From this angle one can see the dark reddish-brown cleft separating the buttocks, the two horizontal folds between the buttocks and the tops of the thighs, the perineum where a delicate fuzz of blond hairs begins, becoming gradually thicker on each side of the slit of the lilac-colored vulva which gapes open, baring a bright pink line. Beyond the rounded pubis the flesh of the belly rises in a gentle curve, dipping down in the middle to form the depression of the navel, which is invisible in this foreshortened perspective. The woman is apparently not bothered by the discomfort created by the damp sheets bunched around her waist, baring the fabric of the mattress higher up on the bed. The rectangle of the window is completely filled by the sky, of a light, uniform blue color, without a single cloud. At the bottom of it there appears from time to time the top of a palm tree swaying in the breeze. The old woman in black has placed the bowl full of blood at the foot of the plum tree and is cutting the skin of the rabbit away from each of the hind paws, a little below the place where the string is tied around them. She then slits the skin longitudinally along each thigh, throws the bloody knife down on the grass, and begins removing the rabbit's skin, rolling it down in somewhat the same manner as one takes off a sock. Below the first equation the boy writes:

$$\frac{S_{A'BC'}}{S_{ABC}} = \frac{\widehat{ABC}}{\widehat{AC}}$$

Raising his head then, he looks at the old woman who has now pulled the rabbit skin halfway down the body. Armed once again with her knife, she detaches the delicate bluish membrane attaching the skin to the flesh and the muscles. Half of the rabbit's body is now bared, so that the pink muscles of the thighs, the hindquarters, and the belly are visible, as in an anatomical plate. Brusquely stretching out the leg whose foot has been resting flat on the bed, the woman causes the door of the wardrobe to pivot round, whereupon it slams against the door frame, bounds backward, and then ceases to move, as the objects reflected in the mirror hung on it are successively swept up in a rapid horizontal movement followed by two briefer ones before they too cease to move. One can now see in the mirror the image of a middle-aged man, with the handsome face and the well-developed physique of an opera tenor, now beginning to grow flabby. He is in his shirtsleeves. The shirt is white, with narrow pink stripes. His tie is dark green. On hearing the door of the wardrobe slam shut, he rises to his feet above the mirror of the dressing table where he was been watching himself make a knot in his tie, turns around in surprise, and raises his eyebrows. The woman has resumed the same position on the bed as before. With her face still turned toward the ceiling she says You bastard. The man frowns, with a surprised and woebegone expression on his face, and says in a voice in the falsetto tenor range Listen I can't do anything for you here I'm not in my own territory as you very well kn . . . Without turning her head, the woman says What do you mean by all that nonsense about your territory do you take me for a fool you've got plenty of influence with the police don't tell me you can't do anything I . . . From time to time a drop of blood, of a deep red, almost black, color now, trickles out of the hole left by the eye that has been gouged out and falls in the grass. The body of the dead animal is jolted by the jerky movements of the two wrinkled hands drawing the skin downward, so that from time to time one of the drops of blood that form in the empty eye socket slides down the muzzle and into the delicate whiskers, where it remains trapped. In the center of the grayish disk projected by the shadow of the magnifying glass on the sheet of tissue paper that the boy has taken out of his drawer and placed on the table after having smoothed out the wrinkles in it, there appears a tiny round spot on which the rays of sunlight that strike the surface of the lens are concentrated. Despite the boy's careful efforts, the hand holding the magnifying glass makes slight movements which produce corresponding slight displacements of the luminous focus that the boy is attempting to maintain on the same spot on the paper. After a moment the paper begins to turn red, and then, as a faint wisp of smoke rises from it, a hole forms, with blackened edges that spread out wider and wider. Hearing another noise somewhere inside the house, the boy quickly shoves the magnifying glass and the sheet of tissue paper back into the drawer of his table, which he then slams shut, and picking up his fountain pen again, he leans over the geometric figure on which, still listening to the sound, he halfheartedly draws another straight line tangent to the circle circumscribed from angle B of the initial triangle. The two boys crouching over with their eyes glued to the tear in the poster on the wall of the barn give a start on hearing the sound of a truck turning into the road leading to the sawmill and lie down flat in the grass. The heads of the umbels sway back and forth above the wavy hair of the wild-animal tamer and on a level with the hat with broad brown checks against a yellow background perched atop the brightly-lighted head of the clown. The noise of the truck dies down. Cautiously raising his head, one of the boys catches sight of it between the leaves of the clump of hazelnut trees, parked near the door of the sawmill. The driver climbs out and disappears inside. The one boy taps the other one on the shoulder and both of them move closer to the barn again, crawling on their hands and knees. The intermingled shadows of the leaves of the walnut tree sweep the surface of the notebook, covering it entirely, moving toward the top, descending again, then gliding rapidly sideways and disappearing. The door at the boy's back opens. The boy does not turn around, apparently absorbed in his work, sticking the tip of his tongue out as he extends with an uncertain hand the straight line that he has just drawn. He can hear the sound of footsteps approaching and is aware of the presence of someone directly behind the back of his chair, leaning over his shoulder and watching him carefully trace a third tangent to the circle, parallel this time to side BC of the initial triangle, as above him a woman's voice utters a few words in a questioning tone of voice, to which he replies only by nodding his head, still without turning around. He is conscious of the gaze that follows his hand holding the fountain pen, which is now quickly writing beneath the first equation:

$$\frac{A'\,C'}{A'\,D} = \frac{\stackrel{\frown}{A\,C}}{\stackrel{\frown}{A\,E}}$$

The voice above him says something else, then there is the sound of footsteps going away, and he hears the door close once again. He then draws a zigzag line in the form of an accordion through the last equation that he has just set down on the paper, listens for a moment to the sound of the footfalls in the hallway, which grows fainter as the feet descend the steps of a stairway. Then after that he can hear the sound of someone walking on the gravel below the window, and then this sound also ceases as there appear successively the hair, the shoulders, the back, and then the entire body of a woman, treading down the grass as she heads toward the plum tree where the old woman in black is finishing skinning the rabbit. He then takes out of the drawer the sheet of tissue paper and the magnifying glass, which he again manipulates, drawing it closer and then moving it farther away, until another luminous focal point forms, from which a thin wisp of smoke soon rises. As they widen, the brownish edges of the hole cause the pink cover of the notebook on which the sheet of tissue paper is lying to appear. Beyond the slit of the vulva, the naked body lying on the bed takes on a brighter pink tinge at the knees, the heels, and the elbows. A long end of one of the sheets that have been pushed back stretches out like the train of a wedding dress over the dark brown rug with a pattern of bouquets of flowers with olive green leaves. Having finished knotting his tie, the man with the fleshy face stands up and says as he looks at himself in the mirror of the dressing table You may be sure that I'll do all I possibly can but. Above his head a grayish rectangle surrounded by a white margin stands out against the wall. The copperplate engraving shows the inside of a barn where a servant girl is leaning backward against a bale of hay, her legs apart, her skirt pulled up to her belly revealing her plump vulva slit open like a fruit. With her arm stretched out in front of her, she is halfheartedly attempting to push away a farmhand who is trying to penetrate her. The farmhand's loose shirt sticking halfway out of his unbuttoned pants forms a pouch of rounded folds hanging down over his buttocks. With one knee bent forward over the bale of hay onto which he has pushed the servant girl, struggling with her to make her lie down completely flat, his position is reminiscent of that of a wrestler trying his utmost to best his adversary, or of Sisyphus straining against the weight of his rock. In the window frame of a gable above the couple, one can see the heads of two laughing young boys watching this spectacle. In their struggle, the two persons below have tipped over a pitcher of milk and a white cat is streaking off in one bound. It is shown suspended in mid-air, its two hind paws extended, its two front paws folded back, its raised tail describing the arc of a circle. Ropes are hanging in garlands of unequal length from the beams of the barn, the end of one of them passing through a pulley and falling in a vertical line. Various farm implements (a pitchfork, hay rakes, a scythe, the chassis of a cart) are leaning against the wall or hung up on it. One can also see a small jug, an earthenware pot, and one of those three-legged stools that women sit on to milk cows. The rakes, the handles of the pitchforks, the legs of the stool still have the curves and wavy lines of the rough-hewn branches they have been made of. A wicker cage is hanging on the wall, just a little above the scythes. The whole, like the plaster on the wall, is colored the same earthen tint, with only very slight modulations distinguishing one object from another. The rear end of a cow appears on the left-hand side of the engraving. Its haunches and hindquarters are covered with a layer of dark, cracked dung. The same pink printer's ink colors the cow's udders, the farmhand's pointing glans, the slit between the servant girl's legs, the tip of one of her breasts jutting out of her shawl, her lips, and her cheeks. A single light yellow tint indiscriminately colors both the bales of straw against which the farmhand has pushed her back, the blond hairs of her pubis, and the curly locks of one of the boys leaning over and peeking through the window in the gable. The farm girl is wearing white stockings rolled around garters, so that they form a round wad just above her knee. Above the curly hair of the animal tamer, a tiger with tawny fur streaked with dark brown stripes and a white belly is shown leaping in mid-air, its two hind paws extended, its two front paws folded back. It stands out against the dark background where, behind the bars of the cage, one can just barely make out in the semidarkness the presence of rows of spectators sitting on the tiers of benches arranged in the shape of a funnel. Black stockings, reaching up just a little past the knee, cover the white legs of the girl, whose feet are clasped around her partner's back. The lips of the vertical slit do not meet, like the edges of a pair of curtains that are not tightly drawn, parting at an acute angle approximately in the center of the circus ring. The couple thus rendered visible appears to be spied on from every direction by the invisible eyes of the spectators, only their bare outlines having been drawn by the artist's brush (heads and shoulders crowded together like flies on a slice of bread and honey), in a thick black stroke. Thanks to another trick on the part of the painter, all the light seems to be concentrated on the heap of tangled, moving limbs of the couple struggling as though in the middle of a ring, which, moreover, the shaft of light sculpts in harsh relief, hollowing it out with dark shadows, illuminating the protruding parts of their bodies (buttocks, backs, thighs) with silvery reflections deliberately highlighted in a thick impasto. The chiaroscuro effects make the two bodies appear to be molded together in a single mass modeled in a soft gray clay, brightened with a pink tinge here and there and glistening with sweat. The whole keeps endlessly falling apart, swelling, forming hollows, and falling back in place again. It looks rather like some smooth-bodied invertebrate animal with multiple members or protuberances, in which violet cavities edged with teeth keep gaping open here and there, as though to bite or let out a rattle or a cry. The heads of stiff hair are tossed back like manes by the furious movements agitating the figures. Various farm implements (a reaper, a tractor, a plow and several plowshares, a harrow, hand cultivators) are stored along the wall, against which there are also piled sacks of fertilizer with an acrid odor and with swelling bottoms on which the names of the manufacturers are stenciled. Copper joints, black rubber belting, and spare parts of machinery are hanging from pegs or large nails. Clods of dried earth and a few tufts of gray grass are still clinging to the blades of the plows and to the bottom parts of the tractor. The moldboards of the plows, like the iron disks of the cultivators, are polished from rubbing against the soil and gleam in the darkness with a cold sheen, like mirrors. Crates, oil drums, greasy rags are scattered about here and there. The sides of the oil drums are stained with greasy spots to which dust has adhered. These dark brown stains partially conceal the green and yellow emblem of a brand of lubricating oil. The floor of beaten earth is also stained with dark spots that become more numerous around the tractor, underneath the crankcase of which is a shiny, darker pool of oil, fed from time to time by a viscous dark-colored drop which collects around a screwhead, swells, elongates to form a pear shape, and falls away. Alerted by a metallic creaking sound coming closer and closer, one of the boys draws his head away from the tear in the paper to which his eye has been glued and raises it, his gesture being immediately repeated by the other boy. Turning their faces in the same direction, they look back over their shoulders and see a straw hat that was once black, but now is a dull, dark gray, emerging from the bushes along the edge of the nearby footpath. A dark-colored scarf running over the crown holds back the wide brim of the hat on both sides of a wizened face, the lower part and the chin of which, with the scarf knotted beneath them, jut out like the jaws of certain breeds of dogs. Gray hanks of hair escape the confines of this headdress and fall over the forehead in a tangled mass, thereby concealing three-quarters of it. For a moment the head topped with the hat seems to glide along level with the upper edge of the bushes, like that of one of those puppets in a marionette show moved along by an invisible hand, proceeding in little jerks along the edge of the miniature stage. Pressing down on the shoulder of his companion to keep him in a crouching position, the bigger boy at the same time whispers in his ear in a low voice She can't see a thing don't move. In the eye sockets, beneath the wrinkled eyelids, there appear a pair of rheumy eyes, with pupils of a faded blue, almost as light in color as the white of the corneas, as though covered by a sort of tiny cloud. As the line of the tops of the bushes descends, there appear in succession narrow shoulders beneath a black work smock with little gray patches, and then the arms. As though to support the body bent nearly double, the bony yellow hands reminiscent of the claws of a chicken are clutching the handlebar of a sort of baby buggy with a wicker chassis perched high up on four metal wheels. The chassis of the buggy is a brownish color. The wicker has shred apart in places and the ragged holes have been carefully mended with string. The metal of the wheels and chassis is rusty. The metallic creaking increases in volume, to a level that is almost unbearable, as the whole of the buggy comes into view, filled with freshly cut grass, bits of which hang over the sides like green hair. A scythe is lying diagonally across the bed of grass, its long curved blade pointing downward between the front wheels. Although the day is far from ended, the sun has already disappeared behind the top of one of the steep sides of the valley. The southern slopes, the meadows across which the river winds its way, and a part of the houses of the hamlet are already bathed in shadow. The four poplars that border the bend in the river begin to tremble, one after the other, revealing the light-colored underside of their leaves, and then they fall motionless again. The woman walks along as though she were blind, her gaze directed immediately in front of her, without hesitating or slowing down, however, as the footpath joins the road coming from the sawmill and leading to the hamlet. The wicker chassis of the buggy leans far over to one side. From time to time a handful of grass topples over, clings to the edge of the buggy, swaying back and forth for a moment and finally falling off, forming a little pile on the white surface of the road along which the black silhouette, seen from the back now, with only the top of the crown of the hat visible between the two shoulders, is retreating in the distance, thrusting out stiffly her feet shod in men's heavy high-top shoes without laces, one after the other, as the piercing creaking sound gradually grows fainter. Rising above the voice of the commentator and the sentimental music, the strident creaking of the wheels of a streetcar rounding a curve assaults one's eardrums like a plaintive, endless cry, dying out little by little, allowing the thundering voice to be heard once again amid the continuous crackling of the projector, booming out the running commentary, a few words of which one is occasionally able to grasp (climate, dream, azure blue, springtime, luxuriant, perpetual), the invisible, barely audible patter of the rain acting as a sort of mute, absorbing the cavernous resonances of the voice, its emphatic and overbearing inflections of a street vendor. In a clatter of rattling metalwork, the front streetcar with the motor unit and the other cars that it is pulling file past at the end of the alleyway. Inside one of the brilliantly lighted cars, one catches a glimpse of the head and torso of a solitary passenger. Distorted reflections of the cheap bar on the corner, then those of the red neon lights of the movie theater facing onto the street run along the sheet metal sides of the streetcar painted yellow. For a brief instant the lights of the streetcar surround with a yellowish halo the vague blur formed by the man and the woman locked in embrace in the dark alleyway. For the space of a second one can thus see the little clouds of breath from the two mouths that are nearly touching outlined against the dark background in the damp, cold air. The reflections of the streetcar windows wheel along the tank of the motorcycle leaning against the wall between the lemonade cases with slatted sides, the little patches of light rapidly growing smaller and smaller as they glide across its curving surface. Beginning to become soaked through, the thin slats of the cases now have dark, irregular fringes as the rain water drips down from their top edge, a dark cherry red against the pale pink, deep aquamarine on the pale blue, emerald on the slats painted light green. As the lights of the streetcar illuminate the darkness, the form of a head and two shoulders appears in black, leaning sideways, its invisible eyes exploring the end of the alleyway, and then the form disappears, as though brusquely pulled away or leaping back into the wings of a theater. The dirty end of the coat that has slid down off the girl's shoulders is now dragging for quite a distance in the blackish mire of clinkers mixed with dirt that the sidewalk is made of. Without ceasing to push before him, so to speak, his inarticulate, wild cries, the clown has now reached the middle of the ring, where he stops dead in his tracks, suddenly mute, in his grotesque drooping costume, amid the roars of laughter surrounding him on all sides like an inhuman rumble thundering down upon him from the walls of the funnel lined with spectators. Beneath the garish grease paint it is daubed with, his face looks as though a gag had been placed over his mouth, as though it were enveloped in bloody bandages smeared with a pale ointment, with the sweeping beams of the spotlights turning the shadows on it a harsh green. For a moment he remains absolutely motionless, his two arms dangling down the sides of his body, his hands hidden by the ridiculously long sleeves of his jacket, his monstrous, bloody face resting on top of the heap of shapeless rags he is dressed in, standing there on his two feet, all by himself. The laughter dies down little by little and finally silence falls once again, still broken from time to time, however, by a woman's nervous titter, half-frightened and half-derisive. The clown then gives another raucous cry, like the bellowing of a wounded beast, which causes another roar of laughter to burst forth from the seats around the circus ring. A uniform layer of blue, as though applied by the brush of a house painter, fills the rectangle of the open window. Except for its color, nothing (no modulation, no unevenness of surface, no hovering cloud, no difference of material or nature) distinguishes it from the walls of the room covered with a uniform coat of paint, so that the solitary naked body still lying on the bed with the rumpled sheets seems to be in the center of an empty space, a cube with smooth walls, closed on all sides, on the surfaces of which there is no shadow, no slight change in tone to indicate the different orientation of the planes, as in those backgrounds of Oriental prints colored in uniform flat tints: simple boxes whose limits are marked off by sliding paper partitions, which appear to be there, fragile and almost unreal, simply to enclose the figures in the scene in a symbolic volume, a ridiculous bit of space propelled through the cosmos by the force of gravity at prodigious rates of speed. The man who is carefully finishing knotting his tie, leaning toward the little slanting mirror of the dressing table, says That man the one named Brown that everybody keeps seeing you with all the time, he's frightfully rich isn't he? The woman lying stretched out on the bed does not answer. Her eyes still staring at the ceiling, her left hand fumbles about on the little night table next to the head of the bed, recognizes the shapes of a package of cigarettes and a lighter, slips a cigarette out of the pack, puts it to her lips, then descends again to pick up the lighter and brings the flame up to the end of the cigarette. The man, who has turned around to look at her, leans over his reflected image once again and smooths his hair down over his temples. When he speaks, it is as if he were addressing his own face, removed from him like a skin and floating in the empty space on the other side of the surface of the mirror. He says But have you ever been interested in any man who wasn't frightfully rich I know very well that people have spread stories about an affair with a jockey. . . . His voice breaks off then and he waits, continuing to gaze with a questioning look into the mirror at the mask of the tenor who has put on a great deal of weight. Then he says As a matter of fact why is it you never got married again: so you could keep the title of baroness? The woman does not move. Her lips exhale a bluish puff of smoke that slowly rises in the dead air of the room. Finally she says Can you pull strings with somebody at the Prefecture or the police or can't you? Illuminated from below by the light reflected from the sea and the flagstones of the terrace in front of the hotel, the ceiling seems as immaterial, as empty, as the rectangle of pale sky or the walls, and the body sprawled out with its legs apart, too pink in certain places, is also totally naked, stripped bare, vulnerable, like the body of a skinned animal. Still standing next to the dressing table, but having straightened up now, the man buttons one of the cuffs of his shirt, contemplating as he does so the slightly sagging breasts with the tender nipples, the thin belly, the delicate fleece between the parted thighs. After a moment he bursts out laughing and says But what wouldn't I be willing to do for the ravishingly beautiful cousin of my best friend from school! . . . From the position he is in, he can see the top of the palm tree that is swaying in the breeze and, from time to time, the bright triangle of a sail drifting slowly past. For several seconds his eyes follow one of the latter, then he turns around and again gazes at the woman lying on the bed. He says How fresh and radiant you used to be Frankly you were dazzling You were . . . His voice breaks off as he continues to look at her. A crooked smile distends her mouth. She is still staring at the ceiling, her eyes wide open, without blinking. The makeup has worn off her face, showing the faded skin underneath, and her lower lip is trembling slightly. Her delicate hand brusquely thrusts the cigarette between her lips, which close round it and grip it tightly, her hand only half-concealing them, her nostrils breathing out two streams of smoke. The man walks back to the window, gazes at the sea, and says without turning around Do you remember the day when you came in with your music case and refused to even look at me? I bet you would never have believed that one day you'd come crawling to me to beg me to. At this moment the image jumps about several times on the screen, which immediately thereafter is crisscrossed with a rapid, chaotic succession of black and white streaks and finally remains completely blank, a dull gray color now, as a broadside of whistles and animal cries rises from the rows of spectators. Coming through the transom of the projection booth, their muffled, disturbing echo rumbles above the alleyway like the sound of a distant riot. In the black mire at the feet of the couple leaning against the wall, one can see a light-colored patch: the white carnation that has fallen out of the man's lapel. The stem of the carnation is wrapped in silver paper. For a moment, thrown off balance by his violent movements, the man's body staggers and one of his feet crush the flower beneath the sole of his patent-leather shoe. The girl's beige coat has now slid all the way down the wall. Her head is still thrown back, wet with rain. As she clasps the man's torso tightly against her with one of her arms, her other hand rapidly descends, takes hold of the member with the crimson head that has emerged from inside her, and raising her thigh higher still, guides the member back into her vagina. The hoots and whistles of the invisible spectators continue. The shadow gradually spreading across the valley reaches the bottom of the eastern slope and begins to climb up along the meadows, but it has not yet reached the edge of the woods. A flock of crows slowly wheels round and round, very high in the sky, at the level of the rock cliff. They describe great sweeping circles that brush the vertical face, off which their raucous cries rebound. With their black wings outspread, almost motionless, they seem to be wheeling around a fixed point, some bit of carrion perhaps, some field mouse or rabbit in its death-agony in a thicket. A circle of people, in which curious onlookers mingle with the hunters, surrounds the body of the boar lying in the courtyard of one of the houses in the village. It is resting on its side, dark and rigid. Its eyes are closed, its snout is smeared with mud, its lips curled back in a frozen rictus bare its powerful tusks of a solitary beast. Beneath its belly and on a portion of its flanks the prickly black bristles are stiff with mud. From a wound in its shoulder there have flowed trickles of blood which are still bright red near the wound but which have congealed lower down, forming brownish crusts, mingled with the mud and the dried sweat that has caused the bristles to stick together in long clusters. A log fire has been lighted directly on the ground beneath the blackened bellies of two caldrons in which steam is beginning to rise from the surface of the water. Children are poking their heads between the legs of the hunters and staring at the dead animal. The hunters are wearing heavy high-top shoes. Two of them have their shinbones protected by leather leggings resembling those worn by cavalrymen. The muddy shoes alternate with the shiny waxed butts of the rifles, the color of mahogany, as the hunters' hands hold the barrels of burnished steel against their thighs. One of the hunters is wearing black rubber boots on which the dried mud of the underbrush has left light gray streaks. Two round patches of the same brick red color as the rubber patches used to repair inner tubes have been stuck on the vamp and the ankle of one of the boots. He is dressed in blue duck trousers that have been tucked into his boots, forming accordion pleats above them. His jacket is also made of blue duck, faded at the seams and at the elbows by wear and many washings. His shirt with wide purple stripes is unbuttoned over his chest covered with thick black hair. His hair curling over his ears, his eyebrows, and his mustache are black. His Mediterranean face with the mat complexion, deeply tanned from being out of doors, contrasts with the ruddy complexions of the other hunters. He winks at the young servant girl who is holding back by the hand a little girl who is eagerly straining her curly head forward to get closer to the enormous felled beast, from which one of the hunters' boots is kicking away a sniffing dog. The young servant girl gives a faint smile and quickly turns her head away, stealing sly glances at the faces of the spectators talking together as they look at the animal. Reassured, she casts another faint, fleeting smile in the direction of the young hunter, then leans her head down level with the child's, says something to her, and walks off, pulling the little girl along behind her. As she walks away, the little girl continues to look behind her. The young servant girl is wearing black stockings, a plum-colored blouse with a small flower print, and a brown skirt beneath which her hips and buttocks sway back and forth. Advancing with hurried little footsteps, their bodies leaning in opposite directions, their free arms outstretched as a counterweight, two men carry one of the caldrons of boiling water over and pour its contents over the boar. The water slides down the stiff hide and flows over the ground, which absorbs most of it, though it leaves a little puddle into which tiny little rivulets continue to drip down from the hairs stuck together, carrying with them a thin trickle of blood that spreads out in the muddy water, twisting and spiraling, enlarging, becoming diluted little by little, forming whorls of a paler and paler pink. Two young boys have slipped in among the first row of the circle of curious onlookers. In their hands are fishing poles and long plant stems on which tiny sticky fish, of a dark gray, almost black color, like patent leather, are strung by the gills. The fish have broad flat heads, almost as large as their bodies. The supple plant stems end in a sort of cylindrical sheath, consisting of seeds set close together, which holds the fish on the stem. A gleaming slime flows from the row of parallel pointed tails hanging downward. One of the boys, having observed the exchange of looks between the servant girl and the hunter with the curly hair, nudges the other boy in the ribs with his elbow and points out to him the silhouette walking away, pulling the little girl by the hand. The pale upturned face of the woman leaning against the wall in the narrow alleyway seems to be floating atop the darkness, faintly illuminated not by the luminous shaft of light that is streaming out horizontally from the transom and passing far above her head, but by the diffraction of its light by the drops of rain that continue to streak it with silvery stripes. At present, the violent thrusts of the man's pelvis as he moves back and forth inside her almost raise her off the ground, crushing her against the brick wall that her head knocks against with each thrust. With her rain-soaked hair dangling down like that of a drowned woman, her blind eyes of a drowned woman wide open in the darkness, she appears to be unaware of the outside world, and the noise of the man's panting breath against her neck relegates to a vague background the various intermittent sounds that seem to be coming from very far away: the noise of the coupling buffers of freight cars bumping into each other, of a locomotive shunting back and forth, of a streetcar rattling along somewhere in the city, and the thundering voice, bursts of which can again be heard through the transom of the booth, the film projection having started up again. The snatches of sentences are interrupted by long silences during which the crackling of the projector can be heard. There is no relationship whatsoever between the monumental power of the voice and the meaning of the words that one can grasp, suggesting a conversation, or rather remarks (for no other voice answers) uttered without anger, in a bantering tone, the few words that the ear catches (time, how much, eat, fortune, Reixach) being pronounced with an interrogative and slightly ironic intonation, booming out like onomatopoeic sounds emitted not by some organ made of human flesh (tongue, palate, lips) but by one of those megaphones, those bull horns with metallic funnel-shaped walls and a rigid tongue in their center, which would not only broadcast them out into the dark rainy night but would also have thought them out beforehand with the aid of a mechanical brain hidden in the base and also constituted of pieces of metal, of multicolored wires, of relays and circuits. Then the sort of trumpeting sound ceases, cut off abruptly, so that one can again hear the continuous crackling of the projector and the rain, punctuated by the hissing jets of steam from the locomotive that is propelling the freight cars along the various switching tracks, as the invisible person with the Cyclopean voice perhaps silently gazes at the face of the actress lying on the bed in order to observe the effect of his last words, pacing about the room perhaps, or lighting a cigarette himself, or, turning his back, leaning out the window for a second time, looking to the right and to the left at the fronts of the luxury hotels and apartment buildings facing the sea in a line running approximately east and west for a distance of over a mile. The succession of façades, the oldest of them overloaded with ponderous decorative motifs, the most recent, a number of which are painted in soft colors (pink, almond green), with balconies stretching out in parallel lines, form an unbroken cliff separated from the sea by a highway where there glide by in a continuous flow in two directions automobiles with gleaming bodies, on the fenders of which there file past in curving lines, reflected as in convex mirrors, the tall palm trees with slender trunks and the exotic shrubs, with leaves reminiscent of sabers or with clusters of white flowers, decorating the median strip between the two lanes of the highway. The rain is still pattering down. The locomotive is now spitting out at more and more frequent intervals its clouds of grayish steam, which turn yellow as the machine passes through the beam of an arc light, stopping, starting up again in reverse, gradually picking up speed. The voice is raised once again, the words (this boy, son, your name, doesn't indicate) roared out by the harsh mechanical voice similar to those of announcers giving a play-by-play description of a soccer match, followed almost immediately this time by other voices (I imagine, must have, father, somewhere, frightfully rich too), then by a silence once again, during which the Cyclops perhaps collapses in an armchair, leaning back or pouring himself a drink, the complicated relays and circuits of the metallic brain collecting during this interval the words of the following utterance that suddenly boom out through the darkness and the rain: high school, exit, picked up by the police, his pocket, drugs? what then? cigarettes? no? worse? damn! The elegant hotels and the most luxurious buildings are strung out in a line less than eight hundred yards long, intersected by a park that is also decorated with palm trees and exotic species of plants. A bandstand with a rococo metallic framework painted sky blue stands in the middle of the park, on the benches of which, between the beds of magnolias, giant yuccas, banana trees, and oleanders, are seated old men dressed in old-fashioned, sometimes threadbare suits and wearing panama hats and spats, and their lady companions with too-heavily painted, wrinkled faces, topped by flowered hats, and scrawny bodies enveloped in yellowed lace dresses and scarves. A steady stream of people in light-colored clothing, in which other stiff-jointed old men meet groups of young people dressed in freakish outfits coming the other way, strolls back and forth till very late at night along the broad sidewalk separating the highway from the beach down below covered with flat round pebbles and bathing establishments with their rows of cabañas, multicolored sun umbrellas, and beach mattresses on which women with splendid, nearly naked bodies tan themselves. Outlined against the glistening surface of the sea there can be seen the dark silhouettes of bathers standing in the foam of the waves breaking just off the shoreline, light-weight boats lifted slightly upward by the ground swell, the sails tinted yellow by the sun shining through them, and the motor-boats towing water-skiers whose feet raise aigrettes of light. Following the contour of the bay, the long line of façades curves gently around to the port, where yachts of all sizes are anchored side by side, their tall varnished masts, the color of honey, swaying back and forth, drawing closer together or farther apart against the clear sky of a uniform blue. Capes, hillsides covered with cork oaks or olive trees, jut out into the sea and surround the city, dotted with villas whose terraces, arcades, or tile roofs are visible here and there amid the green foliage. At the sterns of the yachts the flags of various countries flutter gently in the breeze, red for the most part, or dark blue, above the Anglo-Saxon-sounding names of the boats and their home ports spelled out in gleaming letters that are polished every day, as are the copper rims into which the portholes are set. Beneath the overhanging prows, the reflections of the water form wavy, luminous patterns, endlessly breaking apart and re-forming again. The sea breeze raising the folds of the bright-colored flags also ruffles the feather boas and stirs the mauve scarves of the women with wrinkled faces and thin forearms covered with freckles who sometimes sit on the terraces of the hotels or on the benches along the sea-front, sheltering themselves from the sun beneath violet parasols and holding small dogs on leashes. At the feet of the tall palm trees the automobiles with bodies that gleam like fish continue to meet and pass each other in an endless double stream. On the man's shoulders the black cloth of his rain-soaked jacket glistens in the shadow, reflecting the dim light coming through the entrance to the alleyway. His hips jerk more and more rapidly and a stifled cry bursts forth from between the woman's clenched teeth as the two coupled silhouettes suddenly stiffen in a spasm. They remain locked in embrace for a moment, then the silhouette of the man glides toward the left, detaches itself, takes a few staggering steps sideways, and then, despite the woman's efforts to hold him up, he collapses onto the sidewalk, the woman, who has been dragged down with him as he fell, on all fours now above him, her thighs bared by her raised skirt gleaming like the bellies of two fish, the man's member, also a strange gleaming white, still rigid and crowned with a red strawberry, jutting straight out of the fly of his pants. The woman manages to struggle to her feet first and tries to pull her companion back up on his as he clings frantically to her, muttering a string of curses, sways back and forth, and then suddenly lurching sideways like a crab, the couple stumbles and again falls flat in the mud. The booming voice has fallen silent. In its place, soft music now pours out of the transom of the projection booth. Its inflections serve as a muted accompaniment for the successive falls and the awkward movements of the two silhouettes floundering about at the end of the alleyway, like those little pieces executed pianissimo in circus rings, conducted by the lackadaisical baton of the band leader who has turned halfway around toward the ring, which serve as a facetious sound background for the clowns' acrobatic tricks that fail to come off, punctuated by cruel bursts of laughter from the invisible audience. The orchestration, in which violins predominate, is of the sort used as a background for love scenes (even though the preceding scene between the man and the woman who was lying on the bed makes this possibility rather unlikely) or intense inner psychological conflict expressed by a series of pathetic poses and languid gestures on the part of a person who is all by himself, so that as the two shadows at the end of the alleyway clumsily attempt to struggle to their feet one can imagine the woman, now left all by herself, getting up out of the bed, putting on a negligee, pacing anxiously back and forth in the room, lighting another cigarette, walking over to the open window, contemplating with a blank look in her eyes the animated scene outside, the bathers, the sails, and the motorboats continuing to stand out against the blindingly bright background of the sea like silhouettes in a Chinese shadow play, then ceasing to gaze at this spectacle, and again pacing nervously back and forth across the brown rug, her feet with the painted toenails treading down the leaves and the flowers of the bouquets, the folds of the negligee wafting harmoniously around her long bare legs. In the alleyway, the rain that has fallen is now forming puddles in the potholes in the pavement. It is not easy to gather any precise impression of the disposition of the various locales. The rather large population center appears to have come into being little by little, without any preconceived plan, as smaller towns or neighboring villages grew in size until they joined each other, so that the final conglomeration has the appearance of a disorderly overlapping of urban, rural, and industrial zones, the same arteries being by turn stretches of open highway, then seemingly endless suburban streets, then suddenly lined with lighted stores, passing in front of churches, city halls, bandstands, and then becoming riddled with potholes and running between sidewalks made of cinder concrete, past tract houses, little gardens, and sometimes even fields of beets, and then becoming city streets again, crossing each other, wandering off obliquely for no discernible reason, forming a complicated labyrinth within the sort of chaotic, cancerous proliferation stretching out beneath the low sky on the surface of the flat land, with only a few gentle rises formed by small hills here and there. A canal full of dirty black water runs alongside a complex of warehouses and factories from which there loom up in the darkness metal walkways and jumbles of girders, lighted at rare intervals by electric light bulbs along the pipelines at the foot of the towering slag heaps. Barges that are also black, with varnished wooden cabins the color of honey or mahogany, with portholes set in carefully polished copper rims, are anchored along the banks of the canal. Jutting out over their sterns are flags, in either fiery or funereal colors for the most part (yellow, red, black), whose coarse wet muslin cloth hangs motionless above the names of women (Gabrielle, Germaine, Lily) and home ports with a Flemish ring to them. The public monuments, city halls, churches, and a number of luxurious residences surrounded by private parks are constructed in a hybrid style, an intermingling of Gothic and Louis XIII, utilizing both brick and stone. The bandstands have rococo cast-iron frameworks, painted a pale green. The rain riddles the black water of the canal with closely spaced little circles that overlap each other. The artery into which the alleyway separating the movie theater from the corner bar leads is lined with low houses, seldom more than three stories high, the ground floors of which are occupied by shops, the majority of them food stores: a bakery, a greengrocer's, a bicycle store, a creamery, a hardware store, and the store window of a chain grocery framed in formica of a harsh green color that forms a sharp contrast with the other shopwindows framed in brownish or ocher wood and the dull red fronts of the houses. The lights in the shopwindows are turned off, even those in the chain grocery on the front of which the word CASINO is outlined in yellow against the green background. Besides the regularly spaced lights of the street lamps, only a few rare lighted windows giving off a pinkish or dark yellow glow pierce the semidarkness, and the only fairly large areas that are well-lighted are those illuminated by the lights inside the corner bar and by the neon lights, still turned on even at this late hour, decorating the outside of the movie theater. To the right of the entrance to the movie theater two posters of the same size have been pasted up on the wall, the upper left-hand corners of which have pink bands running diagonally across them, with black letters reading: THIS WEEK and NEXT ATTRACTION. The first of these two bands cuts across a midnight blue background and a row of street lamps with globes strung out like a pearl necklace, by the light of which one can vaguely make out a row of palm trees and pretentious buildings. Sinuous reflections move on the waters of a bay, the edge of which appears to run along parallel to the row of street lamps. In the foreground is the face of a woman who is still beautiful, with an anguished expression. A necklace with three strands of pearls is draped around her neck. Her bare shoulders emerge from a tulle scarf forming the top of an evening dress. Diamonds sparkle on the slender fingers of the hand that she is raising to her mouth in a pathetic gesture. Behind her two men, both middle-aged, are standing face-to-face, one of them with a thoughtful and weary expression, thick lips, and a high forehead, the other with a fleshy face like that of tenors with good-looking features that are unfortunately beginning to sag. Between the two men and the woman there appears the head of an adolescent, which, with its curly tow hair, looks a little like that of a sheep, although the youthful face bears an expression of defiance and rebelliousness. The title of the film is strung out in yellow letters against a background showing a starry sky. The second illustration shows a landscape at night, in which one can make out here and there, dancing in the shadows, little, rather faint beams of light, like those projected by pocket flashlights. The title of the film is strung out in green letters against the dark sky, only a little less dark than the black shapes of the trees or bushes standing out against it above the title. From time to time one of the little cones of light glides over the shiny black surface of the water, reminiscent of patent leather, on which the bushes along the bank are then reflected as the beams sweep past them, suddenly turning them a harsh green. Faint voices, calls, replies in the negative can be heard in the distance, only to be swallowed up immediately by the shadows and the silence, and one can then hear once again the background sound of the summer night with the monotonous, continuous chirping of crickets vibrating in the air. In the foreground, to the left and tilted slightly downward, is the anguished face of a woman, behind whom another woman is standing amid deep shadows, so that she is visible only down to the waist, in a tearful pose, her face buried in her apron which she is pressing against her eyes with both hands. The moon that is rising reveals an impalpable wisp of grayish fog mounting from the river and spreading out over the meadows. In the upper right-hand corner, opposite the corner in which the anguished face is bending downward, in the sky and framed within a yellow halo, the poster shows the two reclining torsos, locked in close embrace, of a man and a woman. The woman's blouse is opened wide, revealing one of her breasts, and her hair leads one to think that this is the same woman as the one shown lower down, sobbing in her apron. With a violent wrench of her hips, the girl breaks away from the embrace of the man who is lying on top of her and whose member floods her thighs, her belly, and the black hairs of her pubis with sperm as it slides out of her vulva, jerking forward violently, in an almost horizontal line, with each ejaculation, the bright red, shiny glans swelling each time as though it were about to burst. The milky sperm flows over the white skin and down along the groin of the girl, who remains motionless, tense and rigid, her legs stretched out now, her head thrown back and turned to one side, as though she were dead, the man's heavy body lying stretched out on top of her, as though he too were dead. One can hear the panting breath of the two of them, the rhythm of which gradually slows down. Bits of hay and straw cling to the brown skirt raised above the girl's hips and rolled around her naked belly. Following the cleft between her buttocks, a little trickle of sperm falls on the old khaki-colored army overcoat of rough material that the man has taken down from a nail and spread out underneath her. The girl suddenly kisses the man on the mouth, holding his head with the black curly hair against hers with her two hands. In the silence of the valley, disturbed only by the continuous sound of the waterfall, the church bell slowly tolls, the vibrations remaining suspended for a long time between the wooded slopes and the cliffs of gray rock. The valley runs almost directly east and west. To the east, its sides join to form a rocky blind cirque, at the foot of which is the source of the river: a horizontal fissure, like a mouth, from which there emerges at the same time an icy breath. Inside the cavern, the rock ceiling slopes downward, becoming gradually darker and darker, until it apparently touches (the darkness at this point prevents one from being able to see clearly) the liquid black sheet of water silently flowing out of the subterranean shadows. From time to time a drop of water falls from the sweating vault of the cavern and produces on the surface of the water a series of concentric ripples that the current carries away. The silence is such that it seems to drown out the sound of the water which, a little farther on, splashes up in twisting whorls, white and roiling, between masses of rocks that litter the riverbed and divide it into a multitude of tiny seething cascades. A bit farther downstream, the banks become wider and the river, whose shallow water flows rapidly at first over a bed of pebbles, gradually slows down and begins to meander through the first tilled fields between the banks lined with water willows and bushes, flowing, transparent, ice-cold, and pure now, over an ocher-colored bottom of tuff-stone, across which the black shape of a trout darts from time to time like an arrow and then disappears beneath the overhanging bank on the opposite side. Later the river tumbles down a first waterfall, then down the one alongside the sawmill, before tracing a large S, the second curve of which skirts the first houses of the hamlet, through the middle of which it then flows, spanned by the bridge. The dwellings, the barns, and the stables are squat build-ings with steeply-pitched roofs. On the side of one of the houses, which in no way differs from the others save for the fact that its plaster finish has been more carefully maintained, is a wrought-iron fence with a gate that opens onto a courtyard beyond which there is a plum orchard that slopes down to the river. Shortly before reaching the bridge, the two boys separate. Holding his fishing pole in one hand, below which the plant stems strung with sticky little fish sway back and forth, the younger boy heads toward the wrought-iron gate which he kicks with his foot and which opens with a creak. Downstream from the bridge are the church, another group of houses, the town hall, the school, and on the right, the cemetery. A few graves are marked with polished marble tombstones, on which family names are inscribed in gilded letters. Others have simple stone slabs. The majority of the graves consist of small rectangular mounds, at the heads of which are planted, sometimes slightly askew, rusty cast-iron crosses with perforated designs. Where the arms intersect there are most often hung one or several of those wirework wreaths with indented edges like the wings of butterflies or insects, decorated with ironwork flowers on which a few purple beads can still be seen. The names of the dead are inscribed in black on little white enamel plaques, most often shaped like hearts, certain of which are also decorated with the photograph of a child's face. Else-where the names are engraved on the open pages of a porcelain book decorated with roses, also made of porcelain, placed at the foot of the cross. Many of these graves are uncared for. Cer-tain of them, however, are planted with flowers: irises, pansies, or climbing roses that cling to the decorations on the crosses. In other places pots, or sometimes just ordinary cylindrical tin cans, have been set around the feet of the crosses. On the sides of the cans turned a reddish-gold color by rust one can sometimes still read the names of brands of canned food, as though they contained some sort of viands brought there, in accordance with age-old rites, to appease the hunger of the dead. Most of them, however, contain nothing but flowers with shriveled petals faded to dull earth tones. Weeds have invaded most of the enclosure surrounded by a low stone wall covered with patches of moss of a green that is almost black. Tiny pink flowers with four petals peek up out of the moss here and there. Only the most pretentious graves and a few of the burial mounds are bordered by bands of gravel that crunch beneath one's feet. Beyond the school, the white cement highway lined with walnut trees on one side leads across the meadows and fields toward the exit of the valley. The man and the woman have now managed to stand upright again. Steadying the man's body against the wall and holding it up with one of her hands, the woman bends down to button her companion's fly with the other and wipe off the mud dirtying his tuxedo as best she can with her handkerchief, after which she starts trying to wipe off the blackish, damp streaks on her stockings and her skirt. The man's head nods as he murmurs confused words. From the vast railway switchyard extending for a long distance behind the wall, beyond the little gardens of the corner bar and the low house alongside it, there can still be heard the intermittent sounds of coupling buffers of freight cars clanging together and those of the jets of steam from the locomotive shunting back and forth. At the foot of a slag heap an electric light bulb seems to draw forth from the shadows the top of a scaffolding made of metal girders, above which is a wheel, taller than a man, that rapidly unreels a cable, also made of metal, then suddenly falls motionless, then takes off in the other direction, again remains motionless for a moment, then begins once more to unreel the cable, at the end of which cages containing men in black work clothes, with black faces and red-rimmed eyes, are descending into the bowels of the earth. It seems as though the movements of the wheel are repeated all night long, like the noises of the coupling buffers and the locomotive. One also hears from time to time the lowing of steers or cows, doubtless coming from a freight car shunted off onto a siding very far away in the rain.

They can be heard now and again all during the night, until morning, until dawn slowly breaks, causing the beams of the floodlights to gradually pale, disclosing the black expanse of roadbed streaked by the cold parallel lines of the shining rails onto which the closed freight cars with sides painted black or a dull earth red are tirelessly shunted by the puffing little old-fashioned locomotive, moving forward and backward, as though propelled by the grayish clouds of steam streaming out from between its wheels.

Walking through the orchard with slow steps, the two women head back toward the house. The patches of sunlight dappled with the shadows of the leaves of the plum trees glide over them. The younger of the two is holding the skinned body of a dead rabbit by its hind paws in one hand, and the bowl full of blood in the other. From time to time the blade of the knife gleams for a brief instant in one of the hands of the old woman, who is walking along bent double, stiffly thrusting one leg in front of the other. Every so often a thick red drop drips off the bloody head of the rabbit and lands on the grass. At the end of each of its paws there remains a little tuft of fur that looks like a bootie or mitten. The boy adds yet another straight line to the geometric figure drawn on the page of the notebook. Below it there are now several equations, all of them crossed out by furious zigzag pen strokes, lying close together like a folded accordion. The sun coming through the window now covers the entire surface of the right-hand page of the open notebook. The head of the old woman, with the ragged straw hat atop it, disappears first, hidden from view by the window sill. Then that of the other woman also disappears, and shortly thereafter one hears their footsteps crunching on the gravel. The rabbit pelt remains in the orchard, hanging by two clothespins from a wire strung between the trunks of two plum trees, in full sunlight. The inner surface of the skin that has been rolled down inside out like a sock is marbled with a network of red trickles that are beginning to turn purple and brown. Flies are already swarming around the pelt. Against the background formed by the dark leaves of the trees bordering the river, they look like luminous dots in the sunlight, describing lines in the air that have sharp, unpredictable bends in them. They alight on the trickles of blood, remain motionless for a moment, then fly off again. It seems as though one can hear the furious buzzing of the biggest of them, two enormous flies, with metallic black thoraxes casting gleaming dark blue reflections. The buzzing grows louder, mounting in sharp crescendos marking the abrupt changes in direction of their flight. The boy hastily pulls out one of the drawers in the table and casts a rapid glance at the dial of the watch lying face up in the middle of a disorderly array of various objects: a box of fishhooks, stamps still stuck to the corners of torn envelopes thrust into the drawer any which way, thumb-tacks likewise tossed in loose, a roll of paper tape, a silk fishing line wound around a bobbin, two balls of chocolate candy, the pale green case of a pocket flashlight, a crushed and wrinkled tube of bicycle patch solvent, the red paint of which is scaling off, a little harpoon made of a brass table fork flattened with a hammer, the tines of which have been filed into sharp-pointed prongs. The bottom of the drawer is lined with a sheet of folded blue paper. The boy raises the paper, thus causing the various objects to slide down it and pile up at the back of the drawer. Underneath the paper is a photograph, torn out of a magazine, of a naked girl with big breasts, kneeling down with her arms resting on her two thighs in the trickling ebb of a wave that has just broken and is spreading out over the sand of the beach. Her round pendulous breasts narrow to pointed tips, like the udders of a nanny-goat. The mounting tide strikes her knees, rising above them and then falling back. Foamy whorls circle her thighs and form bracelets around her wrists above her hands immersed in the water. Keeping his ears open, the boy remains in the same position for a moment, gazing intently at the image, the fingers of his left hand rubbing back and forth across the bump below his belly that gradually grows harder and harder beneath the cloth of his pants, and then he suddenly slams the drawer shut and bends over his notebook. As nothing happens, he opens the drawer again, spreads the disorderly pile of little objects out

over the entire surface of the blue paper, removes the battery
from the pocket flashlight, and finally closes the drawer again
after taking a last quick look at the dial of the watch. Through
the open window there comes the continuous, distant sound of
the waterfall, a muted, sibilant hiss, quite different from the
louder sound made by the overflow of water tumbling down
over the little wall of the millrace above the bridge very close by.
The roar of the waterfall is almost deafening and bounces back
off the rocks, the trees, and the bushes forming a thick curtain
along the riverbank. The two bikes, one with a sky blue frame,
the other black, are lying in the grass underneath an apple tree,
with yellow bamboo fishing poles laid diagonally across them.
The bigger of the two boys takes the battery out of the other
boy's hands and says Can I see? He raises the two little copper
terminals to his mouth and touches them with his tongue. He
says Look, it's dead, and stretches his arm out with the battery
in his hand. The two terminals are of unequal length, tilted sideways and forming an obtuse angle between them. The boy's
tongue has left a few tiny bubbles of saliva on the surface of
them. When his tongue enters into contact with the metal, it
feels only a faint prickling sensation, accompanied by the taste
of copper. The cardboard covering of the battery is red, decorated at the top and the bottom with blue and white stripes. In a
white disk in the center is a blue emblem in the form of the head
of a lion with a thick mane. The two symmetrical fangs of its
lower jaw stand out against the dark blue interior of its mouth.
The wall of the barn covered with posters forms a garish multicolored patch in the greenery, almost at the edge of the woods.
Despite the fact that it is fairly far away, one can make out, on
the other side of the ring where the animal tamer is confronting the tigers, opposite the gigantic face of the clown and coun-
terbalancing it, the head of a lion, approximately six feet high
and a tawny reddish color, roaring and tossing its dark brown
mane. In order to make it stand out more clearly against the
yellow background, the mane is surrounded by a white halo, the

edges of which gradually grow more and more fuzzy. Higher up, the name of the circus is spelled out in large blue letters that form a semicircle above the clown's greenish hat. Above the soft music one can hear from time to time, coming from outside, the louder growling and roaring of wild animals. A heavy smell of dung and of wild beasts hangs in the air beneath the tent. Looking over his shoulder in the direction of the circus ring below him, the band leader, dressed in a tunic decorated with braided frogs and loops, is beating time with his baton, which he is holding between his thumb and index finger, with his little finger upraised, as though to emphasize the faintness, the extreme pianissimo, bordering on complete silence, that the musicians must restrict themselves to. They too are dressed in red, perched on the platform towering above the entrance, framed in crimson draperies, through which the circus performers and the animals enter the ring. Still imprisoned in the dazzlingly bright beams from the spotlights, white ones for the highlights, jade green ones for the shadows, the elliptical sections of which move across the ring along with him, the clown with his face smeared with white and vermilion grease paint on which trickles of sweat gleam is clumsily struggling with a ladder. The ellipses on the ground follow his movements back and forth, lagging slightly behind, then catching up with him, flickering for a moment, not perfectly superimposed, and then stand still. Radiating outward from the clown's feet, two divergent, telescoped shadows repeat each of his movements, amplifying them so that they appear even broader, like two caricatural, gesticulating doubles of himself that have no depth. He has removed his outsize frock coat and is standing there in a dirty short-sleeved undershirt against which his red suspenders stand out clearly. He has not removed, however, either his tie, his collar, his starched shirt front, or his white gloves, which have ridiculously long fingers. From time to time he attempts to push back his celluloid cuffs, which immediately fall back down again, circling his wrists like bracelets. He sets the ladder down on one of its legs and attempts to stand it upright, his jerky movements accompanied by a crescendo drum-roll from the band, as during the execution of a difficult and dangerous trick. Holding the ladder halfway upright with one hand, the clown ceases his efforts and with his other hand makes energetic gestures in the direction of the band leader to thank him and proudly flexes his biceps. As the drum-roll is about to reach its climax, a loud clash of cymbals rings out, causing him to give a start and lose his balance. The ladder that he attempts in vain to hold on to as he turns round and round, as though waltzing with a giant partner, finally collapses on one of his feet shod in long high-top shoes with a flattened vamp resembling a duck's bill. He thereupon emits his bizarre cry once again and hops up and down in one place, clutching his foot and yelping. The audience laughs. At the same time the band leader signals to the musicians to augment the volume of sound, and then reduces it to a pianissimo as the laughter dies down. Sitting on the ground in the silence that descends once again, in time to the beat of the barely audible music, the clown examines his foot, and moaning and groaning, massages his toes beneath the stiff leather of the shoe. Suddenly the tip of it rises, like a jaw with a row of sharp-pointed teeth, emitting at the same time a furious barking noise. The clown gives a start and tumbles backward. Again the audience breaks into laughter. The boy says again But it's dead, I tell you! He jerks the battery out of the other boy's hands and begins tearing off the cardboard covering. The lion's head splits in two and through the tear there appears a gray metal cylinder, half covered with a layer of whitish, gritty particles to which trickles of tar cling here and there. There is also tar underneath the fingernails that are now struggling to make the tear larger. The boy suddenly sucks in air with a whistle through his pursed lips, says Damn! and shakes his right hand vigorously. He says Shit, that really hurts, I've torn off a fingernail. He stops shaking his hand, brings it up level with his eyes, examines it, says once more Shit, that really hurts, shakes it again two or three times, grimacing, then sticks the finger with the torn nail in his mouth, sucks it for a moment, takes it out, looks at it, shakes his hand three or four times more, and sticks the finger back in his mouth, his cheeks forming hollows as he sucks. Without taking his finger out of his mouth he says You haven't got a knife on you, have you? The other boy rummages in his pocket, takes out a jackknife, opens the blade, and hands it to him. The flat handle is made of a reddish material, with a little metallic shield with a guilloched cross decorating one side. The first boy grabs the knife in a clumsy grip, carefully holding to one side the finger that he has been sucking, which is wet with saliva and at the end of which one can see the torn fingernail, edged in black and stained with tar on one side. The dull blade of the knife begins to collapse. The boy looks at the knife for a moment and says Damn is that all you've got?, then thrusts the blade in the tear in the cardboard and finishes peeling it away, revealing the three parallel cylinders constituting the battery. Like the center cylinder, the other two are almost entirely covered with a layer of gritty white particles. He then tosses the knife down and it falls in the grass, and then, with brusque tugs, he separates the three cylinders and triumphantly raises in his hand a strip of movie film isolating the center element from the other two, saying There, you see? The strip of film retains the shape of a U with elongated sides. At the edge of the torn fingernail of his index finger a tiny drop of blood now forms, dark red against the black edge of the nail. Holding his hurt finger to one side, the boy stretches the U out in a straight line and raises it up to look at the sky through the short strip that consists of only five frames and half of a sixth one. After a moment he says Damn, look at that! and the boys' two heads draw closer together. Doubtless it is a scene in which the dialogue is the most important thing, for from one frame to the other no modification, not the slightest shift in the position of a limb, no movement of the actress's head is discernible. On the white sheets of a rumpled bed there lies stretched out the completely naked body of a woman, the upper part of which is resting on top of the mattress cover bared by the sheet crumpled up in compact folds around her hips. The unbleached linen of the mattress cover has longitudinal lavender blue stripes on it. The scene has been shot at an angle tilting slightly downward, from a point situated about three feet behind the head of the bed, thus leading one to think either that the bed has been pulled out into the middle of the room or, more likely, that it is in the center of the bare space on the studio set closed off at the opposite end by a décor made up of panels, likewise completely bare, in the center of which is the rectangle of an open window framing nothing except a cloudless sky of a uniform color, as though applied by a house painter on a canvas situated several yards behind the window. The woman's right leg is bent, with the sole of the foot resting flat on the sheet, and the left leg, which is also bent, is resting on the bed along its entire length, thigh, knee, and tibia. Between the parted thighs one can make out a tuft of light straw-colored hairs. A flat belly extends downward from the rib cage. The slightly sagging breasts have pale tips. The eyes are open in the upturned face, staring fixedly at the ceiling of the room, or rather, the flies above the studio stage with their cables, their winches, their catwalks equipped with floodlights. In accordance with a classical technique, the artist, with the aid of a Venetian red pigment that lightens to a pink tint on the surfaces in relief, has first sketched the body in monochrome, carefully indicating the anatomical details, as in those plates illustrating ancient treatises on painting, showing the modeling of each of the muscles in the form of spindles or sinews that intertwine, cross, and overlap each other. It is only then (just as certain painters sketch in the garments draping their subjects only after having first drawn the nude bodies) that he has painted over this minutely executed preliminary sketch the layer of halftones, of a transparent green, and the light areas, in flesh-colored impasto or pigment the color of mother-of-pearl. Applied in a burst of fiery enthusiasm, the broad brush strokes allow the blood-colored original sketch, which they do not cover entirely, to show through in places. Added with an impetuous, fine-pointed brush, touches of pure vermilion, or vermilion mixed with a lighter color, outline the contours of the toenails, highlight the apricot-colored heels, and brighten the skin at the elbows. Either because the enthusiasm of the painter was captured principally by the body, or because he suddenly abandoned his canvas, he has neglected to overlay the face with pigment, and hence it appears as a blood-colored mass in which the bony structure and the jaws stand out and the bared teeth gleam. One is vaguely aware of the semicircle formed by the technicians (cameramen, makeup men, stagehands, script girls) grouped just behind the camera, invisible though present, motionless in the shadow, their glances converging on the body of the actress. Obeying brief orders, the electricians proceed with light tests, switching various rows of floodlights on and off in turn, and then all of them suddenly blink off at once, the painted canvas representing the sky placed several yards behind the open window is abruptly plunged in darkness, the entire studio set, in the few brief moments during which the director doubtless explains his new orders, being now lighted by only a single bulb which some ladder or framework of a flat has probably knocked against, since it is now swaying back and forth above the bed and tracing, in the hollows and on the reliefs of the belly, the breasts, and the thighs, moving shadows that come and go from right to left, stretching out, drawing back, lengthening in the opposite direction, alternately tracing on one side of the bed and then the other the contours of the outstretched body, in jagged peaks like mountains and curves now gently rounded, now swelling, now jutting out and becoming sharper, standing out in stark black profile before collapsing again. The boy hands the little strip of film over to his companion, and then, rummaging about in one of his pockets with his good hand, removes from it another strip that has retained only a slight bend of the U-shaped curve, and raises it up in turn toward the sky. The five images on it seem to bear no relationship to those of the strip taken out of the battery a short time before (it is possible that they are from another movie), save perhaps the same immobility of the character, a man this time, quite fat and dressed in a dark suit, standing on the red carpet of a room illuminated by a harsh light. With his feet together, he is turning his head to one side, his face thus directly confronting the spectator, as though he were trying to hear some sound or some voice coming from the other side of the door, the handle of which he is holding in one hand. In sharp contrast with the light-colored wall, the dark-colored suit absorbs the light, the whole of it (the folds of the cloth and the edges of the jacket and the vest disappearing) dissolving into a black patch with soft, sinuous contours, like those of an ink spot or one of those silhouettes of birds standing motionless on one leg, hunched up in their plumage, this black patch being surmounted by a pinkish head, with purple blotches on the face and soft skin that hangs down in folds beneath its own weight, emphasizing, despite its flabbiness, the bony ridges of the cheekbones. The torso is bent slightly forward, projecting toward the door the face with half-closed eyes whose eyelids allow his gaze to pass through no more than a narrow slit, with a nose that is not at all prominent, thick lips, and a perplexed, tense, and pathetic expression. The forearm, at the end of which the hand is grasping the door handle, juts out horizontally from the black patch at the level of the belly, like the arm of a gibbet. The garish colors of the postcard (the sky and the sea that are too bright a blue, the façades that are too white, the flowers too bright a red and orange) clash with those of the oilcloth covering the kitchen table on the corner of which the postcard is lying. The gutted and cleaned body of the rabbit is still lying on the thick white porcelain platter. Too long for the platter, the rabbit hangs out over each end, the hind legs over one end, with their booties of fur still intact, and the upper part of the body over the other, the shoulders and the bloody head sagging beneath its own weight dangling down on the oilcloth with yellow, red, and pink checks. Below the rib cage with its scalloped edge, the belly, emptied of its viscera, forms a hollow. On the limbs and the various parts of the skinned body one can see, as in an anatomical plate, the long muscles, swelling out in the form of a spindle, crisscrossing, interlacing, stretching out parallel, or overlapping each other. They are attached to the bones by their sinewy, whitish ends. The whole of the animal seems to be painted in a pink monochrome, darkening to a brick red in the shadows. Reflections the color of mother-of-pearl gleam on the rounded surfaces, on the side toward the open door through which the daylight enters the kitchen. In the bloody head, the one round, glassy eye stares into empty space. Under the table, resting on the stone tiles, an enamel basin, sky blue on the outside and white inside, its edge bordered with a dark blue line, is half filled with the limp mass of viscera with soft folds that are yellowish, pearl gray, pale blue, or violet. Except for the faint ticks punctuating the regular swings of the pendulum that gleams as it passes back and forth behind the glass of the grandfather clock, the only sound to be heard is that of the wings of a dying fly, which vibrate violently, then fall motionless, and then begin buzzing again. The big-bellied case of the clock is painted a chestnut brown. The fly is stuck on a strip of sticky dark yellow paper, covered with the dead black bodies of other flies, hanging from the side of the lampshade in enameled sheet metal which directs down toward the table the rays of light from the electric bulb that has been turned on to combat the semidarkness that reigns in the kitchen, where, with the exception of the door, the daylight enters only through one small window. Doubtless the woman who has laid the rabbit on the table has bumped against the strip of flypaper before leaving the room, for the flypaper, the lampshade, and the bulb are swaying gently back and forth. In the deserted room and the silence disturbed only by the ticking of the clock and the intermittent vibrations of the wings of the trapped fly, the shadows projected by the oscillations of the bulb alternately expand and contract. On both sides of the rabbit a shadow (of a bluish gray color on the porcelain platter, and black when it extends beyond the edge of the platter onto the oilcloth) darts out, outlines and emphasizes the contours of the pink body, and seems to pass beneath it, only to emerge again on the other side, swelling out in sharp humps which collapse again once the light bulb swings back in the other direction. The girl's pink tongue, pointed and supple, protruding from her open mouth set in a more or less frozen smile, comes and goes across the bare swollen glans, of a darker pink, caressing the little hole resembling a blind eye, or licking the mauve ridge. The glance of the girl's dark brown eyes filters through her eyelids half closed by the smile, shifting from the glans to the face of the man, who is now sitting astride her chest, kneading her breasts that his thighs have pushed upward. In order to lick the glans, the girl is obliged to raise her head and bring it forward in a tiring position by straining the muscles of her neck. In order either to aid herself, or to draw the foreskin back more easily and bare the glans that she is guiding toward her mouth, her left hand closes round the base of the stiff member, her little finger disappearing in the black hairs with a reddish cast that it is jutting out from. Without ceasing to brush the tip of her tongue back and forth across the moist strawberry, she places her right hand over the man's left thigh, tugs awkwardly on the waistband of his blue duck pants, pulling them down farther, baring his buttocks completely, and reaches from behind for his balls, which then fill her hand. Having closed the drawer once again, the boy remains motionless, still sitting in front of the open notebook, holding the fountain pen in his right hand as his other hand continues to brush back and forth across the cloth of his short pants, stretched taut now by his hardened penis. As though it had materialized out of nothing, a fly suddenly swoops down onto the page on which the geometric figure has been drawn, the whole of it now illuminated by the sun's rays and of a blinding white color with a faint lemon yellow tinge. The fly remains there for a moment, propped up on its four parted, bent legs, as thin as little wires. It then rubs its front legs together, places them back down, and sits there without budging. Then, passing abruptly from immobility to motion, it advances rapidly in a straight line, cutting diagonally across the tangent A'C', the circumscribed circle, and the side AC of the initial triangle. Having reached a point not far from the center of the circle, it falls motionless once again, and for a second time diligently rubs its two bent front legs together, occasionally passing them over each side of its head that is framed (or rather, almost completely covered) by its two enormous reddish brown eyes rimmed in black. Its tiny proboscis lengthens and contracts in a motion which appears to be synchronized with that of its legs. After a few seconds it proceeds to the right, its new trajectory forming an obtuse angle with the preceding one, intersecting this time side BA, then the circumscribed circle, turning at an oblique angle once again, falling motionless for a fraction of a second, again whetting its legs two or three times, and then, for no discernible reason, returning to the inside of the circle. Approximately in the center of the ring, the clown is now sitting on the ladder resting on the faded carpet spread out on the sawdust. With a perplexed and woebegone expression, he examines his high-top shoe with its gaping vamp studded with nails that resemble a row of teeth. The band continues to repeat the three or four muted measures that punctuate the silence. With infinite precaution, the clown thrusts his hands forward and then suddenly lowers them and places them over the open jaw, one atop the other, leaning down on them several times with all the weight of his torso and flexing his arm muscles, grunting each time like a wrestler, thereafter remaining motionless, his hands in the white gloves still clutching the vamp of the shoe, which he examines from various angles, tilting his head rapidly to the right and left without moving his shoulders, as if it were mounted on articulated rubber vertebrae. The flattened head seems to poke out from the top of the two shadows projected by the beams from the spotlights, alternately thrusting upward and outward. A few scattered bursts of laughter are heard from the audience. Apparently reassured, he finally takes his hands away with the same infinite precaution, and then remains motionless for a moment, waiting expectantly, his eyes never leaving the flattened vamp of the shoe shaped like a duck's bill. Just as he throws his head back, heaving a vast sigh of satisfaction reminiscent of the low bellowing of some animal, the vamp of the shoe, activated by a spring, gapes open again, baring its jaw bristling with nails, as the same furious canine barking sound as before again comes forth from it. The clown falls over backward. The audience laughs. The music grows very loud. The boy's left hand has stopped stroking the hardened glans beneath the cloth of his short pants. His eyes never leaving the fly on the paper, he carefully lays the fountain pen down on the table and his right hand, thus immediately freed, brusquely sweeps over the surface of the notebook. At the end of its travel the closed fist falls motionless against the breast pocket of his shirt. The boy stretches his clenched fist out in front of him, lifts it up to his ear, listens for a moment, and finally disappointedly opens his empty hand. The fly is now resting on one of the panes of the open window, from which it begins a vertical ascent. The tiny black dot moves across the gleaming surface on which the lights and shadows of the trees in the orchard are reflected. When the man lifts one of his hands up from the breast that it has been kneading, one can see the palm of it, of a lighter color than the top, which has been tanned by the sun. The creases of the palm and the folds at the joints of the fingers form sharp black lines, like those in the hands of tractor drivers and mechanics, in which dirty oil and grease become encrusted in indelible streaks. The fingers are blunt, with fingernails that are also blunt and edged in black. The tops of the finger joints are covered with tufts of black hairs with a reddish cast. The skin is of a darker brown than the rough-surfaced nipples of the breasts that appear from time to time as the man's hands move back and forth. Shaped like short corrugated cylinders, the nipples jut out from the center of large swollen areolas, of a paler brown tinged with a bluish gray cast by the veins that flow through them and marble the white skin all around them. Unlike the man's hands, the girl's hands, one of which is still tightly clasping the base of the erect penis, are light-colored on the top, with the reddened skin of the palms furrowed by the sort of very fine little wrinkles, like countless tiny cuts, that tend to become more and more numerous through constant contact with wash-water and wet floor mops. As the camera tracks backward, the two lips of the slit in the circus poster appear on the right and the left of the screen, slowly and steadily moving closer and closer together, concealing as they do so the woman's belly, the man's naked buttocks, the woman's rumpled hair, the pants with folds like an accordion, the forehead, the laughing eyes, the nose, the hands kneading the woman's breasts. Between the two sides of the angle formed by the edges of the narrow slit one can finally see nothing except the glans across which the tip of the pink tongue is gliding back and forth, as there appear, seen from the back, the heads of the two boys with the tousled hair, one above the other, and then their bodies kneeling in uncomfortable positions so that each of them may keep one of his eyes glued to the slit, the hand of one of the two boys buried to the wrist beneath the waistband of his short pants, moving rapidly back and forth, as the camera continues to track backward and the two bodies gradually disappear in the distance, as though they were being sucked backward, becoming smaller and smaller, sucking up along with them the circus ring, the animal tamer with his greased boots and pomaded hair, the tigers leaping in front of the bars beyond which, in the blue half-shadow, the rows of invisible spectators are seated elbow to elbow. There also soon appears the head of the clown, the roaring lion, the tarred wall of the barn, its roof, the edge of the woods, the sloping meadow, the road leading to the sawmill, the vertical poplar trees at the bend in the river, and beyond the trees of the orchards, the first roofs of the hamlet with the church steeple towering above them. To the right of the door of the church is a wooden frame, surmounted by a little canopy a few inches wide covered with a sheet of galvanized metal stripping. Inside the frame the front and back side of a parish bulletin are pinned up with thumbtacks, the former being decorated at the top with a cross surrounded by rays of light, beneath which is a mass schedule written out in a careful round hand with alternating thick and thin strokes, while the back side has a crudely-colored printed illustration showing young boys wearing berets with little metal crosses pinned on them: some of the boys, in the foreground, appear to be marching along singing, and others, in the background, are chasing each other in an alpine décor with meadows, pine forests, and snow-capped mountain peaks. A simple wire grating with hexagonal meshes such as that used for rabbit cages is all that protects the little illustrated announcements, so that despite the canopy above them, rain or dampness has buckled the paper (in particular the sheet on which the hours of the masses are indicated, which must have been pinned up there in the frame for a longer time) dotted with little blisters and yellowish stains. For the moment, the façade of the church is against the light, and its projected shadow extends from the foot of it out over the little esplanade planted with walnut trees where beams of sunlight filtering through the leaves dance back and forth. The fountain is situated a short distance away from the road, and in front of it the frequently trod earth is bare and hollowed away by footprints. The grass covering the surface of the esplanade has two paths running across it, starting from either side of the fountain and forming an approximate isosceles triangle, the two equal sides of which come together at the church door, in front of which there is also a bare patch of dirt in the form of a semicircle whose diameter is slightly larger than the door. The boy furiously rips out the page of his notebook, which does not come out cleanly, the entire left side of it tearing loose in jagged shreds and crenellations. He then removes, one by one, the corresponding ragged shreds that have remained attached to the notebook along the axis of the binding. When he has finished, he makes a little ball of them and wraps it in the page that he has torn out, which he then crumples and lays down on the table to his right. This done, he picks up his fountain pen again, and with the tip of his tongue sticking out, he begins drawing the original triangle and its circumscribed circle once more on the blank page lying in front of him, placing the letters A, B, and C alongside each of the angles of the triangle, drawing the tangent to the circle parallel to side AC and extending the sides BA and BC until they intersect the tangent, labeling the two points with the letters A' and C'. In the deserted orchard, two hens with mahogany-colored feathers are making their way along at a jerky pace, that is to say (since their feet are invisible in the grass), with the upper part of their bodies progressing in a series of movements interrupted by slower movements, thrust their heads out to the right and to the left, warily, halting and quickly pecking at the ground with their beaks, then taking off again, poking their necks forward as a counterweight with each step. A cat with reddish fur follows them at a distance of several yards, also wary, creeping through the grass that reaches up to its belly, its spine flattened, stopping whenever the hens stop, in the middle of a step at times, with one paw motionless in the air, then resuming its forward motion and completing the step it has started taking, like a movie actor when a film that has jammed in the projector begins to move again. The sun strikes the wall of the barn facing the church, on the opposite side of the road which the shadow of the four walnut trees only barely touches. Underneath the huge roof of a reddish mauve color is a door with a semicircular archway above it high enough and wide enough to allow a cart loaded with hay to pass through it. The door is framed with quarrystones that are not covered by the plaster coating of the wall. To the right, suspended from the wide overhang of the roof that protects them, is a row of poles arranged

in a horizontal line a short distance away from the wall, like
those on which ears of corn are hung up to dry, though they
are bare at present. On the double door of the shed, made of
planks of grayish wood, the word C I N E M A is painted in
large ultramarine blue capital letters bordered in yellow on one
side to make them stand out more prominently. The fancy letters look limp and flabby, their ends being rounded and slightly
swollen, so that the I, for example, resembles a tibia. On the
ground, below the poles and along a distance of several yards,
are piled-up logs, the largest of which are split, revealing their
dark yellow sections, which are either round, semicircular, or
wedge-shaped. Tufts of grass are growing alongside the bottom
row, along with a few nettles. Between the top of the pile of
wood and the corn-drying poles, two posters in garish colors
have been pasted on the wall, each of them bearing a rectangular band of pink paper running diagonally across its upper
left-hand corner. On one of the bands one can read the words
NEXT ATTRACTION, and on the other the words THIS
WEEK, standing out against a midnight blue background and a
row of street lamps with globes strung out like a pearl necklace,
by the light of which one can glimpse a row of palm trees and
pretentious buildings. Sinuous reflections ripple on the waters
of a bay, the edge of which appears to run along parallel to
the row of street lamps. In the foreground is the face of a
woman who is still beautiful, with a woebegone expression. A
necklace with three strands of pearls is draped around her neck.
Her bare shoulders emerge from a tulle scarf forming the top
of an evening dress. Diamonds sparkle on the slender fingers
of the hand that she is raising to her mouth in an anguished
gesture. Behind her two men, both middle-aged, are standing
face to face, one of them with a thoughtful and weary expression, thick lips, and a high forehead, the other with a fleshy face
like that of tenors with good-looking features that are unfortunately beginning to sag. Between the two men and the woman
there appears the head of an adolescent, which, with its curly tow

hair, looks a little like that of a sheep, although the youthful face bears an expression of defiance and rebelliousness. The title of the film is strung out in yellow letters against a background showing a starry sky. At the top of the other poster the words NEXT ATTRACTION are pasted over a background of black crisscrossing branches standing out against a very dark gray sky that gradually grows lighter as one's glance descends toward a salmon-colored opening above the horizon. Two men stand silhouetted, like characters in a Chinese shadow play, against the opening, at the edge of a woods. The body of one of them is arching backward, the legs half bent, the head thrown back, the chin pointing toward the sky, one of the arms flexed as though to ward off blows, and the other already hanging down toward the ground, onto which he will soon collapse as his adversary, with one arm curving out in front of him, the fist upraised, is immobilized in that position in which, for a fraction of a second, a body remains frozen after having delivered a violent uppercut. To the right, approximately halfway up the poster, is a long wall of dark red bricks, drawn in perspective, against which, pictured in larger scale and in more precise detail than the silhouettes of the two men fighting, two persons, a man and a woman, are standing locked in an embrace, the latter with her back to the wall. Above the top of this wall one can make out factory chimneys vomiting out black smoke which eventually touches the ceiling of clouds at the top of the poster. In the foreground and to the left is the face of a young woman wearing a bridal veil. Her eyes brimming with tears, her knit eyebrows, the outline of her half-open mouth express despair. The axis of her face is inclined at an angle of approximately fifty-five degrees. At the very bottom of the lower corner one of her hands is shown, pressing the tulle veil against her breast. Immediately next to the face of the woman, the poster shows that of a young man with curly blond hair atop a head resembling that of a sheep. He looks at the young bride with a bored and guilty expression. There is no continuity between the various parts of the poster. The two men at the edge of the woods with the black branches and tree trunks, the long brick wall against which the couple locked in embrace are leaning, and the two faces in the foreground occupying the greater part of the rectangle constitute three different compositions separated by blurred zones, as though they were being simultaneously projected by three machines onto the screen of smoke and black clouds that cause the title of the film, in red letters, to stand out clearly. The figures in the middle distance (the man and the woman locked in embrace) and those, farther away, of the two men fighting are bathed, however, in the very same atmosphere of rain, cold, and dampness, revealed by the wet reflections on the trunks of the trees and the paving stones of the blind alleyway at the foot of the wall. It would appear that it is the same actor, the same adolescent with the head reminiscent of that of a sheep and the curly hair, who is playing in both productions. Dressed in a tuxedo and a pleated shirt front on the poster with the background of bricks and soot, his face leaning over that of the young bride is framed in thick yellow sideburns, like tow, which come halfway down his cheeks. On the other poster his sheep's locks seem shorter; he has shaved off his sideburns and is dressed very simply, in a sports shirt and blue jeans. In order to make out the details of the image more clearly, the boy stretches out the strip of film bent in a U-shape and holds it up to the sky. The transparent body of the actress lying on the rumpled bed then moves upward against the blurred background: first the dark green of the hill, then the luminous blue of the sky in which clouds glide slowly past, changing shape little by little, outlining, filling in, blotting out, and then once again forming curves and hollows in the shape of gulfs, peninsulas, and capes with ruffled edges. The two boys are now lying in the grass. The head and part of the curved stem of a tall grass-like plant sway lazily back and forth, the thin blurred line sweeping at times across the entire surface of the tiny rectangle, the naked body, the rumpled sheets, and the bare panels of the film set. One can smell the fresh odor of grass. When the boy's hands descend, a dark green curtain mounts upward, successively intruding upon the three images. The index finger with the torn nail on which the dried blood has left a brown spot curves slightly inward. A drop of blood of a very dark red color appears to have coagulated and hardened against the blackened corner of the nail. A minuscule oval spot, pale green in color, suddenly appears on the right, a short distance above the bed. Waving the circlet of legs as fine as eyelashes surrounding its body and proceeding in a straight line, it moves steadily across the entire image, at an oblique angle, appearing dark on the naked body and the sheets, and light-colored when it reaches the dark-colored carpet. The boy blows on the insect, and it disappears. Reddish shapes standing out against the background of foliage now cross the room in the opposite direction, that is to say from left to right, following the path bordering the meadow. A bell hung around its neck by a wide leather collar tinkles with a hollow sound at each step taken by one of the cows. The bones of their pelvises jutting out first on one side and then the other, they slowly make their way, one after the other, across the flowered carpet, stand out in profile against the monochrome panel of the set, the cloudless sky framed in the window, of a tint just slightly paler than that of the walls, and then the right-hand panel, and leave the field. As they pass by, their shoes covered with dung overlap the end of the bed turned toward the window. Now and again one of them halts, bites off a tuft of grass on the slope, then continues on its way. Green stems hang out of each side of its mouth, the lower jaw of which moves back and forth from right to left. The transparent body of the woman is still lying motionless, the legs parted. Mingled with the herd of cows, a steer suddenly lumbers along for several yards at a ponderous trot and then, standing on its hind legs, awkwardly attempts to mount one of the cows, which continues to walk along. For a moment they proceed in this way, the body of the steer draped obliquely across the cow's dung-encrusted hindquarters, its two front feet hanging down on both sides of the cow's withers, as it clings to it and tries to keep its balance by stretching out its neck and thrusting forward its pathetic head of an impotent animal with its drooling pink muzzle and its large soft eyes bordered with long lashes. The boy with roughly-cropped hair driving them along lets out violent cries and runs awkwardly after them, hampered by his heavy high-top shoes without laces. The cow then breaks into a trot, kicking its hind legs feebly, and the steer drops back down on all four feet. One can hear the boy's cries booming out in the peaceful air. On being prodded by the pointed stick, the steer also breaks into a trot and passes the cow, which has now halted, with its hind legs slightly parted and its tail upraised, and is loudly urinating. The cloudy yellow stream falls with the sound of a cataract on the stony surface of the path, spatters the hocks covered with blackish patches of dung, and divides into runny trickles that flow down each side of the path, following a sinuous path as it makes its way along the hollows and ruts. The sound of a waterfall, interrupted by silences, bounces off the two parallel walls of the narrow passageway between the movie theater and the brick wall. With his head lowered and one arm bent forward with the forearm resting against the wall, the man vomits in spasms, aided by the woman, who keeps her legs away from the spatters as best she can as she holds his forehead with one hand. A pinkish mass of liquid and half-digested food accumulates in a star-shaped pile between the man's parted feet. Although not as heavy now as a short time before, the rain continues to pour down in regular streams, glistening drops of it whirling about in the pale luminous cones of light below the arc lamps. The woman has drawn the beige coat smeared with mud back up around her shoulders. On the man's bent back, shaken with spasms, the black rain-soaked cloth of his tuxedo gleams in the shadow. From the projection booth there continue to pour out from time to time, in short bursts of sound, fragments of a dialogue, or of a monologue, rather, interrupted by long silences. Even though the voice is still that of a man, it would seem, however, despite the fact that it has the same metallic resonances as before, that it is that of another character, and the words are uttered in a strong foreign accent, either English or American. The second boy has taken out of his pocket the powerful magnifying glass that he has used to ignite the tissue paper, and he is blinking his eyes in an attempt to see the naked body more clearly. Endeavoring to obtain a maximun enlargement, he holds the film at arm's length, moving the magnifying glass close to the film and then farther away. The various parts of the body, the chest, the belly, the thighs, greatly enlarged, are framed in the metal rim that the lens is set in, and glide back and forth with each of the involuntary tremors of the boy's hands, which result in corresponding movements of the image, amplified by the fact that they are enlarged, while at the same time the lines on the edge of the lens curve slightly. There thus file past, moved from left to right, the right thigh that is raised up, the pubis, the left thigh lying flat on the bed, the rumpled, dangling sheet, a stretch of the carpet decorated with bouquets of flowers, and then, appearing on the left of the circle, the broken contour of the light patch formed by the pages of a crumpled newspaper, thrown down on the floor after having been quickly glanced through. The superimposed folds prevent the eye from seeing the whole of a headline in heavy type, though certain words can nonetheless still be reconstructed: (h)IGH SCHOOL STU-DENTS, (im)PLICAT(ed), (d)RUG, and TRAF(fic). In a nervous, uncontrollable movement, the actress lying on the bed unbends her knee and stretches out her left leg, then bends her knee once again in the same position as before, with the left foot slightly behind the right foot, as, without turning her eyes away from the ceiling, at which she is staring fixedly, she fumbles about next to the bed with her hand in order to locate the ashtray, in which she crushes out a cigarette that has burned down only a few fractions of an inch. The hand abandons the cigarette broken in two, the blackened end of which is still smoldering, comes back to touch the left thigh, draws away, and the arm falls motionless along the body, lying flat on the bed, the fingers of the hand where a diamond sparkles opening and spreading apart, closing again, opening once more, then also ceasing to move. The actress then raises her voice. She says Do something for heaven's sake I don't care what telephone or go to police headquarters! The man who has been pacing back and forth across the carpet halts, his two feet together, his torso bending slightly forward, his left hand resting on his back in a gesture of fatigue, his elbow behind his body forming an angle with a rounded apex. His face with heavy features and a high forehead is set in relief by the light from the fixture in the ceiling, which makes his cheekbones stand out and outlines them in black, along with his double chin that hangs down like a goiter over the white collar of his shirt. Finally the thick lips move. The opaque shadow beneath the lower lip moves at the same time and one hears the voice saying in its pronounced English accent You know very well that I'd do anything I could But I'm a foreigner I can't . . . Then the voice dies away and the man continues to stand there, anxious and lost in thought, looking like a large ink spot with sinuous contours. He has halted between the foot of the bed and the window, a little bit to the left of the latter, his face turned toward his right (that is to say, toward the spectator and the bed on which the naked body is lying), his eyes half-closed as though dazzled by the light from the ceiling fixture or perhaps squinting automatically because he is near-sighted, with his head that is thrust forward forming a lighter patch, of a pinkish wine color, that stands out against the rectangle of sky framed by the window, which is of a uniform black, like a coat of paint carefully applied to a wall by a house painter. From time to time the feathery top of a palm tree, of a harsh green color, doubtless illuminated from below by a floodlight, appears above the window sill, sways gently back and forth, and then disappears. The man turns his head the other way, seemingly absorbed in contemplating the dark sky. After a rather long pause, his head slowly pivots back around toward the bed, and blinking his eyelids even faster in order to protect the blinded pupils of his eyes, he clears his throat and says But how about that Lambert fellow that deputy who said hello to you the other day at the Casino, is it possible that . . . At this moment his voice grows hoarse, gradually fading away into inarticulate sounds as black and white patches alternate and collide with each other on the screen, like fragments of broken glass, the rows of faces of the spectators suddenly emerging from the darkness, mere pale blurs, then disappearing again in the darkness, then again illuminated by the reflection from the screen, which is blank at present, of a yellowish white all over, as a chorus of whistles, protests, and animal cries is heard. The overhead light comes on and the indignant faces turn toward the back of the large room, where the film projector is perched on a rough-hewn wooden platform immediately alongside the door of the barn. A man still quite young, with the sleeves of his shirt rolled up past his elbows, his shirt collar open, and his tie unknotted, fiddles with the projector. Without turning around, he waves his hand downward several times in the direction of the spectators, in a gesture that expresses his irritation and at the same time is intended to calm them down. The bare walls of the theater—the inside of a huge barn—are not even plastered, and one can see the surface consisting of gray stones of various shapes (trapezoids, triangles, approximate rectangles) separated by wide mortar joints. Garlands of paper flowers, pink and pale green in color, decorate the place, radiating outward in a star-shape from the middle of a large beam supporting the roof and then surrounding the screen, placed on top of a little stage consisting of a plank resting on trestles. Pasted on the wall to the right of the screen is a large poster on which six long-haired musicians outlined in sepia are standing in a row against a red background. They are equipped with saxophones, banjos, or guitars and are shown in poses that suggest that they are wriggling their hips. Higher up is the word LABYRINTH, in large white letters, the L and the A par-

tially hidden by a yellowish-green band which is pasted diagonally across the poster, and on which the same word is repeated,
this time in black, along with the words SUPER POP FESTI-
VAL. Below it a hand has written SATURDAY AUGUST 4,
with a brush and purple-colored ink. The same green band is
pasted underneath the three letters C, I, and N painted on the
panel of the door, which has been left open to let air in. A burlap
cloth hanging from a frame hides the screen from the view of
people passing by outside. The spectators are sitting on rows of
metal folding chairs, with slatted backs and seats painted pale
green. The audience is made up for the most part of young people and children. Amid the vague commotion, above which there
can be heard a few whistles, directed more in fun than out of
genuine annoyance at the operator of the projector, who is busy
splicing his film, the mooing of a cow in a nearby stable is audible from time to time. Motorbikes, bicycles, and motorcycles are
leaning against the logs piled up outside the barn or the trunks of
the walnut trees in front of the church. The red poster on which
the musicians are swaying their hips back and forth conceals the
lower edge of letters forming the words GRAND PARISH
FESTIVAL. The smell of grass and woodlands drifts through
the warm summer night, intermingled with occasional disagree-
able-smelling whiffs of air from the stables. One can hear the
continuous gurgle of water tumbling over the little wall of the
millrace. From time to time a little breath of air stirs the low
branches of the walnut trees around the fountain. The dim electric light bulb hanging at the point of intersection of the wires
strung from the four tree trunks casts moving shadows of leaves
on the two posters pasted up below the poles for drying ears of
corn. The enlarged and intermingled forms of the oval leaves
sweep across the anguished face of the woman whose fingers
sparkle with diamonds, that of the young bride, the luminous
globes of the street lamps strung out like a pearl necklace along
the bay, and the dark blind alleyway where the two silhouettes,
also dark-colored, with edges surrounded by a halo of light

coming from the street, are performing a sort of pantomime in slow motion which at times brings the two bodies together, causing them to be indistinguishable from each other, and at times separates them. In point of fact, one soon perceives that these apparently random movements are caused by two contrary actions, as the woman clumsily attempts to hold up the drooping, staggering body of the man, who pushes her away, teeters back and forth, clings to her once again, and then pushes her away again, propping himself up with one hand against the brick wall first, and then against the piled-up lemonade cases, gradually attempting to make his way toward the entrance to the blind alley. Between each of what might be called not embraces but rather, in the language of the boxing ring, clinches (when one of the adversaries who has been knocked half unconscious clings to the other and thus immobilizes his arms), during which the two silhouettes merge (an obscure mass with four intertwined legs, from which an arm emerges now and again, acting at times as a counterweight, groping about for support in the void, at times upraised as though to deliver a blow), the woman pulls her coat that is sliding down back up around her shoulders. Finally she takes advantage of a moment when the man has withdrawn a short distance to quickly thrust her arms through the sleeves, and then hurriedly stumbling over the uneven paving stones to support the man again, holding him up with one of her hands placed underneath his armpit and the other clutching his forearm. They make their way along in this fashion for several yards, the man's body bent slightly forward, leaning on that of his companion, his unsteady legs getting all tangled up, his knees giving way beneath him, until finally they reach the end of the alleyway and emerge from the darkness, standing up straight now beneath the light of a street lamp that reveals the disorderly state of their dirty, rain-soaked clothing, and, hanging half way out of one of the pockets of the woman's coat, the pink cloth of a pair of nylon panties hastily thrust inside it. As she holds the man upright beneath the lamppost, the woman begins, with the aid of the pair of

panties rolled up in a ball, to remove as best she can from his
tuxedo the mud and the traces of vomit with which it is spattered.
The man with the sheep's head continues to mutter, protesting
and flopping about, feebly attempting to free himself, and then
suddenly, taking advantage of the fact that the woman is bending over to wipe the filth off her own stockings, he pushes her
away with a violent shove, so that, losing her balance, she totters backward, twisting her high heels, as the man turns away and
starts across the road, crossing it very fast at an oblique angle, in
a nearly straight line, heading toward a sedan parked almost directly across from the bar against the opposite curbing, and then
stands there with his two legs apart, clutching with his left hand
the handle of the front door, decorated with a bowknot of white
tulle tied around it, as his right hand feverishly rummages
through his pants pocket, the woman in turn hurrying in his direction across the road whose paving stones glisten in the
rain, then stopping dead in her tracks, hobbling backward, and
kneeling down to try to disengage the heel of her right shoe,
which has caught in one of the streetcar tracks, her head turned
back over her shoulder toward the man, crying, You're nuts, you
know, you must be absolutely nuts getting soused like that,
you're nuts, do you know that?, her clear voice, raucous with
distress and indignation now, rising in the quiet hissing of the
fine rain that continues to fall on the long deserted artery, the
gray pavement, the slate roofs, and the pitch-dark façades. His
attention attracted, doubtless, by the noise, a grayish silhouette
stands out against the ocher background of the clouded window
of the bar. Inside the edge of the shadow one can make out the
torso of a man dressed in black leather and wearing a cap, surrounded by a yellow line cast by the light illuminating him from
the back, which repeats the outline of the silhouette. The shadow
of the torso grows smaller and more distinct and that of the head
eventually coincides with the contour of the man's real head as
he presses his face against the windowpane and peers outside
between the advertisements for brands of apéritifs or juniper

liqueurs pasted on the glass. The nearby lamppost sheds enough
light on the advertisements so that one can see their bright colors
(yellow and red, green, white and red), forming a contrast with
the dull monochrome area within which the blurred silhouette is
standing, in front of the gleaming reflections on the sides of the
bottles above the counter of the bar. Hopping about on one leg,
her other leg bent back with the foot level with her knee, the girl
puts her shoe back on. The shadow on the windowpane moves,
grows larger, glides to one side, and disappears. Still sitting on
the ladder and continuing to clutch the vamp of his shoe with one
hand, the clown, turned toward the entrance to the ring, gestures
repeatedly with his hand in the direction of a figure who is
finally heading his way, followed by a beam from another spotlight. This person is dressed in a royal blue swallow-tail coat, with
gilded metal buttons. His bearing, his face devoid of makeup
express the sort of reserve, at once contemptuous and respect-
ful, characteristic of servants in great mansions or headwaiters.
His hair, slicked down with pomade, shines like that of the
animal tamer. Reaching the clown's side, he bends over and attentively watches the latter's little pantomime as he points to his
shoe with his free hand, then squeezes his hand into a fist, as
though crushing something, repeating the gesture several
times. The man dressed in tails nods, heads back toward the performers' entrance, disappears behind the velvet curtain, reappears almost immediately, and walks over to the clown, holding
out to him an object that gleams in the glare of the spotlights.
Emitting his wild cry, the clown seizes it, and is about to clamp
it around his shoe, but then stops and examines the nutcracker
that has been handed to him. Frowning, he turns it round and
round, looking at it from every angle, and then, dumbfounded,
lifts his face with the downturned mouth up toward the man in
tails. The latter spreads his hands apart, pretending not to understand, and then, clenching his own fist, repeats the clown's gesture of squeezing the shoe, pointing down toward it with his left
index finger. The bizarre yelp again comes out of the paint-

smeared mouth, the words You must be a little nuts, aren't you? rising in a hoarse cry, the end of which is drowned out by the bursts of laughter from the audience, accompanied by loud rolls from the bass drum. The man in tails gives a sudden start, spreads his hands apart again and says Come come Mister Chewing-Gum, you did ask me for a nutcracker, didn't you? There are three shadows on the floor of the ring now: the two divergent shadows of the clown and that of the man in tails lighted from the beam of a single spotlight which casts part of his face in deep shadow. Their actions synchronized with the spoken dialogue, the three flat telescoped silhouettes move back and forth across the faded carpet making agitated gestures, the amplitude of which is distorted by the spotlight. The clown cries I asked you for a nutcracker but now I'm asking you if you aren't a little nuts yourself! The audience laughs. The face of the man in tails freezes in an expression of polite stupefaction. He begins a sentence but is interrupted by the funnyman who cries Oh dear oh dear oh dear, twirling his index finger in the white glove round and round repeatedly against his temple and rolling his eyes. Then in pantomime he shows his partner how ridiculously small the nutcracker is in proportion to the enormous shoe. In so doing, he has let go of the vamp of the shoe, which suddenly snaps open again, this time letting out a roar as loud as that of a lion. The man in tails gives a start and leaps backward, miming utter terror. The clown, dumbfounded, does his best to muzzle the gaping jaws, and struggling to hold them down as they jerk upward, cries A real nutcracker, not a dinky little toy one, you nut! Oh dear oh dear oh dear, you must be a little cracked!, whereupon he straightens up in fury and leaps toward his partner, holding in his right hand a leash, at the end of which is a collar running around the vamp of the shoe, which opens and closes, barking like a dog with every step he takes, as the audience bursts into laughter, the bass drum rolls and the cymbals clash even more loudly, and the man in tails flees at a run and disappears behind the drapes, which continue to sway back and forth as the clown, stopping dead in his tracks and facing toward them, shrieks in his hoarse voice You big ugly mug you!, then amid the laughter from the audience, walks back with jerky footsteps and waggling hips to the center of the ring, followed by his two distended shadows, his feet spread apart, his right hand holding the end of the leash accompanying the movements of the shoe with the gaping jaws that he is leading along like a puppy-dog, talking to it in a soft voice. The shadow has not yet reached the gigantic face daubed with red and white grease paint, the animal tamer putting his tigers through their paces, and the head of the roaring lion. The sun's rays make a rainbow in the mist of little droplets that rises and hovers in the air at the foot of the waterfall. The concentric bands, violet, indigo, blue, pale green, yellow-orange, and red hang suspended, iridescent and transparent, in the fine, luminous mist. Standing on a rock, the boy takes a big breath and pinches his nostrils between the thumb and index finger of his right hand before diving, feet first, into the basin at the foot of the waterfall. For a moment he appears to be suspended motionless in the air, with one hand on his nose, his two legs spread apart and his knees flexed, as though riding an invisible mount, above his reversed image on the lacquered surface of the water, into which he disappears in a splash of foam, his head bobbing to the surface almost immediately, his hair stuck to his head like a skullcap above his forehead. From the rock that he has dived from, on which the other boy is already standing with his toes gripping the wet moss, one can see the first boy's body, colored a greenish white by the water, standing out against the deep blue of the basin, his legs alternately stretching out and bending back, like a frog's. The clear voices and calls of other youngsters ring out, mingled with the sound of the waterfall. Crouching for the leap, the second boy now dives in too, head first, but falls flat on his belly in the water, which this time frames the plunging body like two silver wings with claws curving inward, gleaming for an instant in the sun, then falling back in droplets. The first boy runs along the riverbank and begins climbing up the rock again on all fours, already pinching his nostrils as he rises to his feet at the top and without pausing plunges into the water again, diving sideways this time, however. The shadow of the trees growing along the edges of the waterfall spreads out over part of the basin, dotted with luminous patches dancing on the surface. The boy scrambles out of the water, stumbling on the pebbles along the bottom and using his hands to help him. He joins the other boy, who is now standing in the sun, shivering, with his teeth chattering. The wet skin of the two thin bodies is dotted with little drops of water and covered with goose flesh. One of the boys says Damn, that water's cold enough to freeze the balls off a brass monkey! The two of them stand there like that for a moment, their teeth still chattering, looking at the other youngsters, unable to keep their limbs from trembling. Their dripping bathing trunks droop down, baring their bellies down to the pubis and revealing their narrow hips and the muscles of their abdomens. After a moment one of them turns around, and walking along the riverbank, reaches the rock and again clambers up it. However, instead of diving back into the water, he continues his ascent toward the top of the waterfall, bent double, almost on all fours, clutching the branches of the bushes. Beneath the delicate skin of his back, his spinal column forms a line of little bumps and the soaking-wet bathing trunks reveal the top of the cleft between his buttocks. The other boy, who has followed him up the rock, says Where are you going? Without interrupting his ascent, the boy makes a sideways gesture with his arm, as though to signal to the other boy to keep quiet. His companion follows him. In the shadow of the leaves, their milky skins are again tinged a pale green. The little patches of sunlight slide across the surface of them, making the drops of water glisten as they pass over them. As the two boys climb higher and higher, the shouts of the youngsters splashing around in the basin below them become fainter and are eventually drowned out by the sound of the waterfall as they progressively catch glimpses of the stretch of river upstream, the fields and the meadows along both sides, the roof of the sawmill, and the white strip of paved road leading away from the village. A black form, bent double, appears between the last trees of the orchards, walking along the path. Beneath her drooping skirt two feet stick out, shod in men's heavy high-top shoes without laces which her half-bent legs thrust forward alternately in a jerky shuffle. The bent silhouette is leaning with both hands on the handlebar of a baby buggy with a wicker chassis perched high on the wheels. One cannot hear the creaking of the rusty hubs. From time to time one can see the gleam of the curved blade of the scythe lying diagonally across the buggy, with the blade hanging down toward the ground between the front wheels. The wicker chassis of the buggy is empty. With her shoes back on again, and running awkwardly in her high heels, the girl crosses the few yards that separate her from the car and grabs the hand of the man, who has finally managed to pull the car keys out of his pocket. She says again You're a little nuts aren't you don't you realize you can't even. Clinging to the car door handle with his other hand, the man draws back and raises his arm, the gleaming little keys dangling from his hand. As he does so, he pulls toward him the body of the woman, who is still holding on to the raised door handle with both hands, and as the two of them collide, his own body begins to fall over backward. He staggers for a moment, his lower back arching forward, without letting go of the handle, however, and then, with a force that one would not have expected in view of the drunken state he is in (or perhaps, on the contrary, it is multiplied tenfold by the alcohol he has consumed), his body suddenly slackens like a bow that has just launched an arrow, violently catapulting the girl, who stumbles forward and grabs hold of the hood of the car. As she has hurtled by, she has bumped into the radio antenna, which continues to oscillate, causing the grayish rain-soaked tulle ribbon dangling from the end of it to sway back and forth from right to left. Taking no more notice of the woman, the man bends over, reaches with his right hand toward the car door lock, and swears loudly. With a brutal shove he pushes away the girl, who is again attempting to hold on to him, swears at her, and then, letting go of the door handle, begins inspecting the ground alongside the car, muttering to himself. For a second time the curtain over the windowpane of the bar is raised and the shadow with a cap on top is first outlined in gray against the yellowish background, then grows smaller, and finally coincides with the chestnut-brown spot formed by the face with its nose pressed against the windowpane between two advertisements for apéritifs, and then the shadow grows larger again and the curtain falls back. The long deserted artery stretching out into the night is illuminated only by the globes of the street lamps, spaced alternately along both sides, punctuating the darkness with little islands of light which reveal the reddish or violet-colored façades of the buildings and gradually grow fainter and fainter toward the edges. Between the lampposts are long stretches of dark shadow. One can no longer hear any sound coming from the projection booth, now too far distant, but the intermittent sounds of the coupling buffers bumping together and the jets of steam from the locomotive can still be heard above the rain. On all fours now, taking no notice of the mud, the man leans his head to one side along the paving stones and inspects the area underneath the wheels of the car. The woman goes back over to him, and grasping him under the armpits, tries to help him to his feet, urging him on in a half-whisper. He escapes her grasp with a shrug of his shoulders, and without changing position, lifting his leg up to one side like a dog, gives her a sharp kick in the shins. The woman stifles a cry of pain and moves away out of reach. Still pushing her baby buggy with the scythe attached to it, the old woman dressed in black is now halfway between the hamlet and the barn. Still on his knees, the man fumbles about in the left-hand pocket of his pants and manages to extract a cigarette lighter from it. The flame illuminates his hand from behind, encircling his fingers and palm with an apricot-colored line. It also causes the sheep mask, glistening with rain, crudely blocked out in black and pink between the two-colored sideburns and the curly wet locks hanging down over the forehead, to suddenly leap out of the shadow. One of the ends of his bow tie which has come undone drags on the ground as he lies down flat again, his face turned to one side, with one of his cheeks almost touching the paving stones, his hand moving the flickering flame of the cigarette lighter back and forth underneath the crankcase. After a moment the flame goes out and the young man with the sheep's head raises himself up, swearing. Still prudently keeping her distance, the girl says something to him in a conciliatory tone of voice, waving her arm in the direction of the bar several times in a gesture of invitation. Taking no notice of her, he walks alongside the car as the girl rapidly retreats around the hood, ending up on the opposite side of the car, where she halts, standing there motionless, as meanwhile the man too goes around the hood, but without paying any further attention to her, totters up onto the sidewalk and proceeds unsteadily off down the avenue, the girl in turn starting walking again, following him at a distance of several yards, and then, encouraged doubtless by his lack of any sort of reaction, quickening her pace, catching up with him, putting one arm around him to hold him up and placing her other hand beneath his armpit, whereupon she is suddenly propelled sideways like a puppet, and then, as she stands there with her bent arms raised in front of her face, protecting herself as best she can from the hail of badly aimed blows now raining down on her, their two black silhouettes are suddenly surrounded by a halo of fine silvery little raindrops in the headlights of a car, the two of them gesticulating in a grotesque manner, the young man's arms flailing about like windmills, the girl's back bent, the entire scene then abruptly disappearing from view, the darkness closing in again as the taillights of the car grow smaller in the distance and the sound of the wet tires grows fainter as behind them the double furrow of little plumes of water that they have raised sparkles brightly, then disappears, then sparkles brightly again in the next lighted stretch, and finally disappears altogether. With his back turned away from the spotlights, the dark silhouette of the clown stands out, surrounded by a silvery halo in the beam of light in which myriads of impalpable particles swirl about. With a horrified and dumbfounded expression, he watches the man in the royal blue swallow-tail coat walk toward him, followed by two ring attendants carrying an enormous cardboard nutcracker painted a metallic color. Bursts of laughter are heard from the tiers of benches as the clown leaps back in terror, getting all tangled up in the leash leading from his hand to his foot, tumbles over backward, turns a somersault, and lands on all fours, like a dog, with his face turned toward the man in tails and a colt revolver in each hand, his yapping voice rising about the bursts of laughter as he cries out hoarsely, Halt, whatintheworld is that?! At the sight of the revolvers, the man in tails gives a start, halts dead in his tracks, and signals to the ring attendants to halt too. He says But Mister Chewing-Gum . . . , his voice being immediately drowned out by that of the clown, who barks Stay right where you are! and waves the revolvers threateningly. Holding his hand out in front of him with the palm vertical, as though to protect himself, the man in tails cautiously advances one step, bends down, picks up the tiny little nutcracker lying on the carpet, raises one of his feet, pantomimes the gesture of squeezing his own shoe with it, scornfully tosses the little object away, and pointing first to the huge cardboard nutcracker that the two ring attendants are still holding up and then to the clown's enormous high-top shoe with the gaping vamp, repeats in pantomime, twice this time, the squeezing gesture. The clown struggles to his feet, looks fearfully down at his shoe, raises his head, points the barrel of one of the revolvers in the direction of the giant nutcracker and screams You're a little cracked yourself, aren't you? The bursts of laughter from the audience and the loud rolls from the bass drum prevent one from hearing what the man in tails answers as, with a supercilious expression, he begins his pantomime all over again, picks up the little nutcracker, thrusts it forward into the light, tosses it aside, and points to the gaping shoe and the giant nutcracker, whereupon the indignant yap again rises above the bursts of laughter, like the screech of an exotic bird, at once plaintive and furious, not simply pronouncing but shrieking the words You want me to kill my doggy? The man in tails gives a start and says Your doggy? But listen, Mister Chewing-Gum, you . . . , then leaps in terror, as do the two ring attendants, on hearing the furious barking sounds that emerge from the gaping shoe, emphasized each time by a twitch of the shoe and the hand holding it on the leash. The bent black silhouette of the old woman, who has now reached the barn, passes in front of the tearful face, painted red and white, which appears to emerge from the grass. At present, despite the roar of the waterfall, one can hear the continuous, strident creaking of the wheels of her baby buggy, which gradually disappears, as though she were sinking into the earth, her skirt, her torso, her face eventually being hidden by the slope lined with bushes, above which the straw hat moves along for a few yards more, and then also disappears. The two boys are crouched down, their bare bodies squatting side by side in the dense thicket of bushes and little trees growing above the waterfall. Although still out of breath from diving, swimming, and clambering up the steep slope, they are absolutely motionless, frozen in the position of scouts on the lookout, save for their sides and their ribs that show beneath their tender skin, rapidly rising and falling. They crouch there, panting, their backs bent in parallel curves, their faces leaning forward, the quiet hissing sound of their rapid breathing escaping from their mouths, like athletes trying to catch their second wind or hunters fascinated by their prey and petrified with excitement. With infinite precaution, the boy who has gone ahead first parts the supple branches with his hand. Through the ragged, nearly black screen formed by the tangle of foliage in the dense shadow of the thicket, the water of the river flowing slowly along before it tumbles down the waterfall sparkles brightly between the little islands of tuff-stone with clumps of sage or broad pale green leaves, like little flaring ruffs, clinging to them. The leaves of two slightly parted, nearly horizontal branches of a young oak tree stand out against the dazzlingly bright background. Their sinuous contours cut it up into bright areas that interlock, like pieces of a jigsaw puzzle. A reddish patch that shines like fire in the sun suddenly moves into one of these fragments. Stirred by the breeze, the branches make slight motions, rising and descending, crossing and then drifting apart, by turn concealing and revealing the hair, the face, the shoulders, and the arms of a little girl standing behind a bush. Her very white, milky skin seems to concentrate the light, or rather, as in overexposed films, to have a faint luminescent glow, as though it itself were a light source. The face framed in the flaming orange-colored halo is dotted with freckles. With awkward gestures, casting rapid glances all around, the little girl pulls her arms inside her blouse, where they move about clumsily. A kingfisher with dark blue wings on which the sun casts dazzling reflections darts along, swift as an arrow, just above the surface of the water, avoiding with a slight flicker of its wings the little islands of vegetation and disappearing upstream. There are clumps of pink and mauve flowers, with long stems that run along horizontally for a little way, then curve upward toward the light, growing between the stones of the little wall that deflects part of the current in the direction of the sawmill. The little girl is now holding the front of her blouse in her teeth, her arms and hands continuing to move underneath it. In the shadow at the edge of the thicket where the two boys are squatting, insects like spiders, with long legs spread wide apart, allow themselves to float slowly along on top of the calm water, motionless and weightless, as though resting on the surface of a mirror, and then suddenly moving a short way upstream in swift little darts, then again falling motionless, drifting with the current. On the undersides of the leaves of an alder whose lower branches hang out over the water, the reflections form luminous patterns that continually ripple, break apart, and re-form. Almost entirely hidden by the vegetation from prying eyes on the opposite bank, from where the two boys are watching, the little girl's body is visible down to the waist. Above the glistening surface of the water, two dragonflies with their long abdomens coupled together hover in one spot, as though suspended from an invisible wire, surrounded by the sparkle of their wings. The cries and calls of the youngsters from the bottom of the waterfall can still be heard, mingled with the muted sound of the cascading water, punctuated from time to time by the plop of a body diving into the basin. Fatigued by the crouching position that he is in, the second boy squats back on his heels, like a monkey, and a dead branch cracks with a faint snap beneath his feet. The boy who is holding the branches apart with one hand makes a furious downward gesture behind him with his free hand. Stretched taut over their buttocks because of their crouching position, the boys' bathing trunks drip slowly, little trickles of water running down over their ankles and gliding across their feet. Somewhere or other a bird lets out a few brief cries, materializes on the stem of one of the pink flowers, which bends slightly beneath its weight, and remains there for a moment, swaying back and forth, turning and leaning its head abruptly right and left. Its plumage is smoke gray, its breast orange. As suddenly as it has alighted, it flies away, giving a series of strident calls in close succession. Bending once again as the bird takes off, the flower continues to sway back and forth for a moment. Little by little the breathing of the two boys frozen in their crouching position slows, so that their ribs and their sides move only very slightly now. However, either because fatigue causes their muscles to tense, or because in the shadow where the two of them are crouching they cannot manage to warm themselves, their limbs continue to tremble. In addition to the roar of the waterfall, one can hear the murmur of a rivulet of water falling between two rocks into one of the little basins staggered like a flight of steps just upstream from the waterfall. Its bottom, consisting of little pebbles and sand, undulates below the concentric ripples that form on the surface of it. On hearing the strident cry of the bird, whose wings brush past her, the little girl has given a start and fallen motionless. Holding the front of her blouse between her teeth and rolling her eyes fearfully, she again casts swift glances all about her, and then suddenly making up her mind, she opens her mouth, allows the blouse to fall from her teeth, and hastily puts her arms through the shoulder straps of a bathing suit, though not quickly enough for there not to be visible for the space of an instant one of her barely-formed breasts, of a sudden dazzling white in the sunlight, with a little pale pink tip. The bathing suit has wide red and white horizontal stripes, and the neckline and shoulder straps are edged in red piping. The two boys give a sudden start at the sound of a voice very close by, just as the head of a fat man with a black mustache and bulging eyes emerges from a tuft of vegetation a few yards away from them, soon followed by his torso as the taut curve of a fishing pole rises in the air. The torso is clad in an undershirt that bares the man's huge pale arms, ending in two hands with tanned skin, causing him to appear to be wearing gloves. His thick white neck is intersected by a sharp dividing line, above which the wine-colored tint of his face begins. The man is speaking to a woman, who until now has also been invisible behind the thicket of river willows, and whose head, followed by her torso clad in a dark blouse, now suddenly appears alongside the little girl. One of the boys says Geez! and scampers off into the woods, the other boy at his heels. Dead twigs snap beneath their feet and branches scratch their sides. Amid the sound of their heavy breathing and their hearts pounding in their chests, it seems to them that they can hear shouts behind them. Running as fast as their legs can carry them and without turning around to look, they cross the meadow above the waterfall and plunge into a field of corn. The long leaves stir around them with a harsh rustling noise. They continue to run between two rows, then the first boy turns at a right angle, crosses through five or six rows, and falls motionless, in a crouching position. For a moment all they can hear once again is their loud panting breath and the dull thudding of their hearts. As these latter gradually slow down, they begin little by little to perceive the faint sound of the long leaves rubbing together as a puff of wind stirs them, and the buzzing of insects. The ears of corn are sheathed in green husks at the ends of which tufts of silky light brown or reddish vegetable hairs hang out. No echoing voices can be heard now from the direction of the river: only the same unending sibilant sound of the waterfall as always. One of the boys says Do you think he recognized us? The other boy is busy licking his finger and rubbing it across a long gash running across his side. He shrugs his shoulders and says The trouble is, we have to go back and get our fish poles and our duds. He cautiously raises himself upright until his eyes can see above the tops of the cornstalks. In a meadow, upstream and to the left, the old woman in black is cutting grass with stiff but precise motions. There is no one in sight along the line of bushes and trees at the top of the waterfall. The shadow descending the southern side of the valley is beginning to reach the meadows farther down the slope that extend from the edge of the woods to the river. Standing on the sidewalk in the suburbs of the city, the girl watches the silhouette walk away at an unsteady pace, hugging the brick façades of the houses and the shops with closed shutters or lowered iron grilles. Finally she shrugs her shoulders, turns around, and crosses the road in the direction of the bar, the door of which is now open, framing the massive bulk of the man in the leather jacket. With his head turned to one side, his gaze follows the person who is walking away, disappearing almost completely in the areas in deep shadow, then reappearing at intervals, looking smaller each time, in the widely-spaced areas of light around the lampposts, then disappearing again. On catching sight of the man in the leather coat, the woman pauses for the space of an instant, but then continues walking toward him. Without turning his head, the man draws aside to let her past. Having reached the doorstep of the bar, she stops there instead of going inside, and starts to speak. Beneath the shadow cast by the visor of his cap, the man's face is invisible. It is impossible to say whether he is listening to what the woman is telling him. After a moment, however, he slowly turns his head toward her, looks her up and down, and then, still not saying a word, he reaches his hand out toward the pink silk panties hanging out of her coat pocket, into which she has hastily stuffed them. His face expressionless, his eyes lowered, he grasps the silky material between his thumb and index finger and slowly pulls on it until little by little all the cloth stuffed in the pocket comes out, inch by inch at times, and at other times emerging from the edge of the pocket in crumpled wads, the man's hand continuing to rise, still pulling slowly, the billowy folds coming loose, the last bit finally sliding out, the lights in the bar showing through the transparent bit of pink cloth which continues to swing back and forth at the end of the man's half-raised arm, the hand rising just an inch or so more, so that the girl's arm, suddenly shooting out, grasps only empty air, the man's arm, stretched all the way up now, holding the bit of pink cloth very high as it continues to sway back and forth, the woman, at a disadvantage because she is shorter, climbing up on the doorstep too, stretching her arm out again and leaping clumsily, her body bumping into the man's, her hand again clutching only empty air, and finally the bit of pink cloth ends up on the sidewalk, where the man has not even thrown it down, but merely opened his fingers, the panties, still swaying back and forth, floating past the woman's drenched hair and falling on the shiny black asphalt in a pathetic, ridiculously small pile, the woman looking at them for a moment, bending down to pick them up, then abruptly straightening up, clinging to the shoulders of the man, who has pivoted around, facing toward the left now, one foot already at the bottom of the step, his eyes searching in the distance for the silhouette that he has lost sight of, suddenly frowning, the features of his face growing taut, just as the silhouette, minuscule now, slowly emerges from a dark area, stumbling along, brightly illuminated for an instant and then melting into the shadow once again as the man in the leather jacket, his head still turned toward the end of the long street

and deaf to the woman's torrent of words, gently and effort-
lessly, as though he were dealing with a child, removes her hands
from his shoulders, clasps her two thin wrists in his right hand,
and still with no apparent effort, draws her, or rather, although
his various movements appear to succeed each other with the
same absence of haste or violence, pushes her inside the bar, the
woman taking a few clumsy steps across the floor, her torso bent
forward, her two arms outstretched as though the man were
still pulling on her wrists, though in fact he has stepped away and
is now walking toward the alleyway, from which he emerges a
moment or so later, pushing in front of him the big motorcycle,
which he calmly straddles, his foot pressing down several times
on the starter, the motor suddenly backfiring and then starting to
turn over, beginning to move off down the street as though it too
were staggering, the man's two feet propping him up on both
sides allowing him to regain his balance, until finally he turns to
the left, and picking up speed, quickly disappears amid the roar
of his motor, the sound of which dies out very rapidly, the girl,
who is again standing on the threshold of the bar, listening to it
fade away, and then, when it has stopped, shrugging her shoulders once more, looking for a moment at her torn stockings in
the light coming from inside the bar, turning around, and closing
the door behind her. Doubtless the camera has been hoisted up
to the very top of either a church steeple or one of those scaffold-
ings of metal girders that rise above the pit of a mine and over-
look the entire urban complex, but in any case along the axis of
the long artery, for one sees this latter from a steep plunging
angle, faintly lighted here and there by the lampposts. On
the dark surface of the screen, the urban complex looks like a
shadowy beach, the lights of which dimly outline in widely-spaced
dots the chaotic network of streets between the houses, all just
alike and all the same height, the warehouses, the factories
along the canal full of stagnant water where the reflections
scarcely move. On the deserted avenue one can just barely make
out, far in the distance, the little black patch that now and again

leans with one hand against a wall, slows down, stumbles on, disappears, crosses another lighted area, still clumsily lurching
along. Projecting ahead of it its jiggling bowl of light, the
motorcycle rapidly covers the distance separating the two men.
Once the motorcycle rider has arrived within some twenty yards
of the man he is pursuing, however, he slows down and stops. He
lifts the heavy machine up on the sidewalk, parks it on its stand,
and then continues on foot. The interval between the two men
diminishes from one lamppost to the next. Having arrived at this
point in the story, which also marks the end of one chapter, the
woman stops reading. Doubtless the air coming through the window that opens on the black sky has now turned a bit cooler, for
she has pulled the top sheet covering her legs, her belly, and her
bosom up farther, so that only her shoulders and her two bare
arms are now visible. With one of her ringed fingers inserted
between two pages at the place where she stopped reading, she is
holding the book face down on the bed, with the title against the
sheet, so that only the back cover, on which the titles of other
works in the same collection are listed, is visible. With a worried
expression she contemplates a few faint freckles dotting the
back of her hand, the skin of which is smeared with lotion and
beneath which the raised veins are beginning to show. On her
ring finger is a gleaming emerald surrounded with diamonds
which she distractedly turns this way and that so as to catch the
light and sparkle, her attention elsewhere, her ear cocked in the
direction of the next room, from which snatches of a telephone
conversation can he heard. Sitting, or rather, buried, in an armchair next to a little round table, the man in the dark suit, with
the vest buttoned from top to bottom despite the heat, is holding
the telephone receiver up to his right ear. He is leaning forward
in a position that betrays a certain tension, his feet touching the
base of the armchair, his legs bent back, his knees apart, his left
forearm resting on his left thigh, his left hand dangling between his thighs, his right elbow leaning on his right thigh, his
face turned downward toward the red carpet and almost entirely

in shadow, with only the very tip of his flat nose protruding. It seems as though the artist has started over several times before being satisfied with the final results, having first painted the face turned toward the right (that is to say, toward the little table on which the base of the telephone is resting), as can be seen from a profile scraped out with a knife (or perhaps one should interpret this flat patch where the color of the wall shows through, barely altered by the layer of paint that has been scraped away, an area which, moreover, is larger than the head itself, as merely the shadow of the latter, projected by a low lamp situated to the left of the figure), and then, a second time, in its final position, that is to say, seen in three-quarter profile, the face bathed in a violet-colored half-tone. When he changes position, the harsh light of the ceiling fixture gliding over his face reveals, in black and pink, his heavy, drawn features, as through an unconscious reflex he turns his head toward the base of the telephone, as though to bring himself face to face with his invisible conversational partner, his features being thus suddenly projected forward, though his eyes remain in shadow, as though staring into space, their gaze at once empty and steely, as if his eyes were listening too, closely watching something that is happening not outside himself but in the synapses of his brain, along which the tenuous, nasal sound sputtering in the receiver is passing. Thrusting one leg out from under the sheet and stretching it out, the woman touches with her toe the mirrored door of the wardrobe standing next to the bed, causing it to pivot on its hinges until there appears in the narrow rectangle delimited by the two vertical sides the blotched face, reflected now in quarter-profile, that is to say: the silvery hair (where here and there a few yellow locks can still be seen), the wine-colored nape of the neck, the thick, flabby neck, with folds of flesh hanging down over the collar of the shirt, the circumvolutions of the ear, of a lighter rose color, and the sinuous line starting at the arch of the brows which forms a hollow just below, then curves out at the cheekbone and then droops in soft folds lower down. As it has pivoted, the mirror has reflected for a fraction of a second the half-shadow of the studio where there have appeared, in a brown monotone, the dark shape of the camera with the multiple lenses, its film reels, its base, its cables, and the attentive though blurred faces of the film crew standing in a group behind it. The decrepit old film projector suddenly makes an abnormal clicking sound as on the screen the face glued to the receiver moves jerkily from one position to the other, like a series of freeze-frame shots, beginning with the initial position of the head, seen almost directly from the back at first, then in quarter profile, then in profile, then in three-quarter profile, whereupon yet another storm of whistles, protests, and animal cries arises in the hall, which, though it dies down almost immediately, nonetheless prevents one from grasping the words escaping from the lips of the man, now shown full-face, the projection having resumed normally. One then sees the right hand hanging up the receiver, the heavyset man getting up out of his armchair and lumbering over to the door between the two rooms, halting motionless in the doorway, the end of his already-begun sentence emerging little by little from the hubbub of protests so that once silence has fallen again, one can hear, pronounced in a strong English accent, the words: very friendly, could put in a word with, police commissioner, understanding . . . , the woman lying stretched out, the book with her index finger inserted in it still lying on the bed alongside her, her gaze riveted on the black rectangle of the window, saying after a moment How much?, the man waving his hand with a nonchalant gesture, the woman saying Those swine, the man repeating the same gesture, the woman then angrily striking the book lying flat on the bed several times with her hand, saying Don't you see the whole thing was a put-up job All that Lambert fellow wanted He's a vulgar He's going to I'm going to . . . , then falling silent, lying there motionless once again, the sheet that the violent movements of her arm have caused to slide down now baring her left breast, without the thought occurring to her to draw it back up again, the man too falling into his familiar pose once again, one hand on his lower back, as though to ease the pain in it, one elbow bent back, his torso leaning slightly forward, as though bending beneath the weight of his heavy head turned to one side, contemplating the half-naked body with his pathetic, strained, myopic gaze filtering through his half-closed eyelids until his thick lips move once again, the voice with the strong English accent saying You should try to sleep now do you want me to get you those pills?, the voice of the movie director then shouting Cut, and the floodlights going out one after the other on the invisible catwalks in the shadows of the flies that gradually shut. For a moment one can hear the bustle of equipment being shifted around, the director's voice commenting on the camera angles or giving orders, and the discussions of the technicians preparing to carry them out. The English actor has sat down on a folding chair, behind the camera and off to one side. Dismissing with a single word the makeup girl who has approached him, he sits there, slowly wiping his forehead and temples with the towel he has grabbed out of her hands, nodding in agreement with the words of a young man (an assistant?) dressed in a pink and green checked cowboy shirt with the shirttails hanging out over his pants, who is addressing him, leaning down toward him and supporting himself with one hand on the arm of his chair. Then the young man straightens up and the actor sits there all by himself in the great vastness of the studio, the limits of which (the dirty walls, the roof above the catwalks) disappear in hollow shadows where sounds of hammers, creaking noises, and booming voices echo back and forth. A multitude of cables in rubber sheathing snake across the floor and intertwine in a disorderly tangle. The actress is still lying stretched out on the bed in the same position, and the makeup girl whom her partner has sent away is bending down over her face and delicately passing a soft-haired brush over it. One of the stagehands who was just about to empty the contents of the ashtray lying on the little table at the head of the bed into a sack suspends his gesture at an order from someone and busies himself placing the three crushed and twisted cigarettes with the blood-red ends back in the porcelain saucer. When the rows of floodlights come on again one after the other, the viewfinder has been rolled forward again and in the frame there appear in the foreground the head, the torso, and the arms of the woman who is leafing backward (doubtless searching for a passage read too hastily or a detail that she has not paid sufficient attention to) through the book that she has stopped reading a few moments before. The little bell indicating that shooting is about to begin again has just fallen silent when there comes from outside the sound of two cars that seem to be chasing each other, honking loudly, drawing closer together, then braking and skidding to a halt, and as the doors that have been thrown open are still slamming shut, the first of a band of young male merrymakers bursts into the bar where there are three persons: a fat woman with a mustache busy wiping glasses and carefully putting them back on the shelf in a row, a barmaid about twenty years old, dressed in a pink blouse and a black skirt, conversing across the counter with a huge man in a leather jacket and a cap, leaning on his elbows with a glass in front of him. The bar is lit by two frosted glass globes hanging from the ceiling that cast a dim light on the walls covered with yellowed wallpaper with vertical stripes enclosing a repeated pattern of little bouquets in dull colors. Against this dark background there stand out the advertising posters for brands of apéritifs or juniper liqueurs, some of them totally abstract, in harsh contrasting colors (red, black, and white; green, red, and white; yellow and blue), others showing bottles with labels in gaudy colors, a zebra against a blue and red background, or a woman's face with red lips, topped by a hooded cape decorated with cherries. An enameled cast-iron stove, the pipe of which runs diagonally across the room, emits a faint bit of heat along with whiffs of tar that mingle with the smell of juniper, wet plaster, and the sawdust scattered in untidy piles on the floor. The tops of the tables are made of a dark yellow wood, with darker crescents and circles here and there left by the bottoms of wet glasses. Above the counter a neon tube casts its pale light on the puffy face of the fat woman, the barmaid's chestnut brown hair with a mahogany-colored cast to it here and there, and the gray cap of the man in the leather jacket whose face disappears in the shadow of the visor. All but one of the newcomers, who is wearing a tuxedo with silk lapels, are dressed in navy blue suits, brightened up with ties in loud colors, and have white carnations in the buttonholes of their lapels. They all have long hair that falls over their ears and the backs of their necks, as wavy and straw-blond as wigs in some cases, and slick and shining with pomade in others. The hair of one of them has a definite reddish cast. That of the young man dressed in a tuxedo is a pale yellow, as curly as wool, and his sheep's face is framed in thick sideburns of the texture of tow, which are also pale yellow. They all seem more than a little tight, speak in loud voices, and jostle each other as they elbow their way through the door. One of them heads straight to the jukebox standing against one wall, already fumbling in his pocket, bending over to examine the titles of the records, slipping a coin in the slot, and pressing a button, whereupon a roar of sound with a strong beat bursts forth in the narrow room, deafeningly loud, wild music, as anachronistic and incongruous as the gleaming chrome of the jukebox standing in front of the moldy wallpaper, next to banquettes with little tufts of horsehair sticking out through the holes in the brown moleskin. Raising their voices to a still louder pitch in order to be heard over the hubbub, three of the young men lean their elbows on the bar as two others, their legs bent at the knee, carefully re-comb their hair, smoothing their ducktails down with the aid of little tortoise-shell combs that they have fished out of their pockets, bending their backs so as to bring their faces down to the level of the mirror running behind the counter below the shelves. After having cast a brief glance in their direction, the barmaid with the silk blouse seems to lose interest in them and continues her conversation with the man in the leather jacket. The fat woman has leaned her elbows on the bar counter, her arms spread apart. Her sleeves rolled up to her elbows bare her pale, soft skin. Her palms and pudgy fingers, of a bright pink color, are furrowed with fine, deep wrinkles, like scars, set close together, and her shiny face is frozen in a mechanical smile. Between the folds of her eyelids her tiny eyes, brown and watchful, look as hard as bits of glass. She says in a cordial tone of voice Good evening to the bachelor party, what will you have to drink?, then, without waiting for the answer, as though knowing in advance what it will be, stopping the barmaid from coming over to help her with a shake of her head, she places six glasses with thin stems topped by a little inverted cone in a row on the counter. One of the young men gives the bridegroom several hearty claps on the shoulder, shouting Your last night as a free man! The last time we tie one on together! We've got to drink to that! The young bridegroom's eyes carefully avoid the barmaid's. The wag of the party says Six?, then points his finger first at the fat woman herself and says Six plus three makes nine, right? Isn't that right Lily? The barmaid interrupts her conversation with the man and starts to say something, but the fat woman motions to her to keep still, and impassively begins immediately to line up three more glasses alongside the first six and fills all of them. The wag pushes two of the glasses over to the barmaid and the man, raises his own glass in their direction, shouting Cheers! We're celebrating his last night as a free man! and tossing his head back, swallows the contents in one gulp, after which he slams his glass back down on the counter, and with a sweeping gesture of his hand that includes all those present shouts at the fat woman Another round of the same for everybody! The man in the leather jacket begins to make a gesture, but the barmaid puts her hand on his forearm, and then picks up the little glass and raises it in turn in the direction of the young men, her eyes avoiding the bridegroom's, however, and wets her lips. The fat woman gathers up the shards of the little glass whose stem the wag has shattered when he slammed it back down on the counter

and says You don't have to break everything you know! The wag
fumbles around in his hip pocket, takes out a packet of bills,
peels one off, slaps it violently down on the counter, and repeats
the same sweeping gesture, shouting Never mind about your
damned glasses This is a bachelor party and we're celebrating!
The other young men applaud loudly and shout at the tops of
their lungs. Two of them come over to clink glasses with the
barmaid and raise them in the direction of the man. After placing another glass on the counter and whisking the bill away, the
fat woman fills the little cones again. Arriving at the one sitting
in front of the man in the leather jacket, which he has not yet
touched, she murmurs a few words to him with a shrug of her
shoulders. The man also shrugs his shoulders and swallows down
the contents of his glass, which she immediately refills. The
bridegroom looks at the girl and turns his eyes quickly away
when hers meet his. The wag says Drink up everybody come on
you lovers let's all have a drink let's have two!, and comes over
to clink his glass against those of the barmaid and the man, spill-
ing half of his and shouting None of that now everybody drink
up! The other young men clink glasses, shouting full blast, and
also come over to clink glasses with the barmaid and the man
in the leather jacket. The wag grabs the young bridegroom by
the shoulders and pushes him over to the barmaid, bawling out
It's his bachelor party Everybody drink up! The young bridegroom and the barmaid touch glasses and their eyes meet. The
barmaid's gaze is absolutely expressionless. Another young man in
the party then slaps another bill on the counter. The young bridegroom and the barmaid continue to stare into each other's eyes.
Behind her, in the mirror, one can see the yellow headlamps of
cars glide by from time to time, though less and less frequently
now. Still staring at the young bridegroom with her expressionless gaze, the barmaid raises her glass and drains it, whereupon
she turns away and resumes her conversation with the man in
the leather jacket. One of the young men in the party has
plopped down on a banquette, and with his head on his crossed

arms resting flat on the table, appears to be sleeping. The wag shakes him, shouting Hey Pierrot, you okay? The young man raises his head and opens his bleary eyes. The wag leans over a little farther and makes him swallow the contents of his own glass. The barmaid looks at the bridegroom again, and turns her eyes away. The fat woman fills the glasses once more. The young men are talking more and more loudly and their shrill voices mingle with the din from the jukebox, which the wag keeps putting coins into, planted in front of the machine and leaning on it, his arms spread apart, his fingers keeping time on the chromed sides of the jukebox and his foot tapping. Above the glass set on an inclined plane, beneath which one can see the records stacked up vertically, is a long rectangular panel which has lighted up when the music first began blaring forth. Made of colored glass, it shows a bay of a midnight blue hue stretching out in a long curve bordered by a series of façades with pretentious decorations. A play of lights gliding slowly along the curve appears to represent the headlamps of cars moving in single file down a highway lined with tall trees planted along the edge of the water, which is also colored a midnight blue, and on which a yacht painted white is sailing, all lighted up, as one after the other the roman candles of a fireworks display rise in the starry sky, red, yellow, and green, following divergent curves, bursting, and falling back down in umbrella-shaped showers of sparks. Amid yet another storm of protests and animal cries that fills the barn, the projector starts up again, a series of blacks and whites follow one another rapidly on the screen first, and then, for a brief instant, one can read the words POLICE COM-MISSIONER BASTIANINI (doubtless the title of the film), followed by the number of the reel, letters and figures that disappear almost immediately, whereupon the screen becomes completely black as the sentimental music grows louder and then dies down little by little, soon forming merely a sound background for a voice that emphatically shouts a commentary, a few words of which are comprehensible (jewels, pearls, paradise, millionaires), accompanying the slow shifting, against the black background, of an unbroken string of lights outlining the contours of gulfs, peninsulas, capes, and jetties that glide from right to left. On the shadowy beach, nothing on either side of the luminous festoons allows one to distinguish the sea from the land, except, from time to time, a liquid reflection that repeats the line of lampposts along the shore, the headlights of a solitary car, and at infrequent intervals a few blurry patches of light. Everything seems deserted, uninhabited, or abandoned, like a theater emptied of its audience, the careless electricians of which have forgotten, on leaving for the night, to turn off the old-fashioned outside decorations, consisting of clusters of light globes that closely follow the principal lines of the invisible architecture, pediments, a cupola or a rotunda. One after the other, very slowly, the luminous pearls are blotted out by the rigid edge of the airplane wing, at a slight oblique angle to the left-hand side of the screen, also black in the blackness, on which there gleams at regular intervals the faint reflection of the little red bulb blinking at the tip. At times the sparkling string of lights surrounds on three sides the geometric form of a yacht basin. The plane is flying at too high an altitude, however, for one to be able to make out the thin spindle shapes of the yachts lined up side by side, with portholes set in polished copper rims, with decks washed down each day with bucket after bucket of water, with tall masts the color of honey or mahogany swaying very slightly against the black sky. Little by little the garland of pearls separates into strands, joins up with others coming from inland, the luminous dots drawing closer together and bunching up, until there appears in the distance a sort of whitish, vaporous incandescence perforated by flickering beams of light, in the thin mist above the sea. Surrounded on all sides by shadows, the blurred, blazing island, where here and there glittering lights like diamonds blink on and off, drifts along, strange and solitary in the black emptiness. The voice offscreen alternating with the waves of sentimental music, in which violins predominate, continues its commentary, the volume of which is so amplified by the scratchy loudspeaker that one cannot grasp the meaning of it, though one's ear catches a few isolated words here and there: casino, fever, banco, dawn, lights, growing pale, night, ending. The strands of a pearl necklace appear in three superimposed tiers, against a black background. As it tracks backward, the camera reveals the velvet pedestal shaped like a headless neck cut off at the shoulders. Other similar pedestals, likewise covered in black velvet, display diamond rivières or necklaces of precious cut stones; still others, in the form of cylinders, have platinum bracelets, minuscule wristwatches, or gold chains around them. On the gleaming glass of the shopwindow and superimposed on the jewels displayed in it there appears the reflection, from the rear, of the dark, transparent silhouette of a man with a huge body, his head crowned with silvery hair combed straight back. It is daylight. Beyond the silhouette there glide by the reflections of long cars with brightly-polished bodies, following one after the other along the highway. A leather briefcase dangles from the man's hand. One of the cars slows down and stops along the sidewalk, and the transparent silhouette begins moving, seemingly receding among the emeralds, the pearls, and the diamonds and becoming smaller and smaller as the man crosses the sidewalk and stoops over to get into the car whose invisible driver is holding the door open. The car takes off and the camera lingers for a moment on the display window, the entire screen being filled by the black and mutilated forms of the torsos or arms on which the jewels sparkle. The following sequence of shots must have required particularly careful planning on the part of the director, for it involves a series of complicated movements of the camera, which draws closer, then moves away, then again draws closer, successively framing: a black leather briefcase with a metal clasp, then the two protagonists sitting on a banquette like those found in a bar, then one or the other of their faces, and finally the briefcase again, open this time, however, so that one can see the inside of it, stuffed with packets of bills. One of the two characters is the heavy-set man with the thick lips, the short nose, and the high, bare forehead with the hair combed straight back. He is still dressed exactly the same as always, in the dark suit with the buttoned vest. With his torso supported on either side by his arms, the palms of his hands resting flat on the banquette, his gaze reduced to a slit between his half-closed eyelids, he has not touched the contents of the glass sitting in front of him and is listening, with an inscrutable expression (weariness, disgust?) on his face, to the voluble words of the other character whose profile makes him look like a bird, with a prominent hooked nose, bushy eyebrows, and a thin mouth. The latter is dressed in a light-colored suit, without a vest, the jacket of which is open, showing the front of a soft pale blue shirt and a tie held in place by a metal clip. He is sitting in a careless, non-chalant pose, with one of his arms across the back of the bench, and his other arm emphasizing his words with rapid gestures, in the manner of Mediterranean peoples, his free hand turning round and round, like that of a prestidigitator, at the end of his arm that keeps moving back and forth. He seems self-assured and loquacious, and yet at the same time slightly anxious, turning his head around frequently as though to keep close watch on the entrance to what must be the back room of a bar rather than the bar itself, a room that is apparently deserted, at a slow hour (doubtless chosen deliberately) in the middle of the afternoon. The heavy-set man remains impassive, still seated in the same position, not saying a word. It would be impossible to say whether he is listening or not. Once more the head of the bird-man abruptly pivots from left to right toward the entrance to the room, and then, making up his mind, with that disconcerting rapidity of conjurers his hand suddenly appears above the brief-case, holding a few little paper bags that have unexpectedly materialized in it. The camera draws closer and the man's open palm occupies the entire surface of the screen for an instant before the hand abruptly closes again and thrusts the little paper bags in the pocket of the fat man's suit coat. Still sitting in the same position, the latter merely motions with his chin toward the briefcase placed between them, the rapidly turning hands then opening the little clasp, and, after the man with the bird's head has cast another rapid glance over his shoulder, raising the flap of the briefcase. At this point, as the camera moves closer, the briefcase in which the hands are rapidly counting the packets of bills seems to move directly in front of the spectators, becoming larger and occupying the entire surface of the screen once again. In the next series of shots the fat man is still sitting in the same spot on the bench, but he is now all alone. He has a drowsy look about him, his eyes half-closed, seemingly unaware that his partner has disappeared. After a moment, however, he moves, throws a bill down on the table, rises ponderously to his feet, and walks over to the door to the lavatory on the right. In the harsh light flooding the little room with tiled walls, the flesh of his face appears to sag even more. Reflected in the mirror above the washbasins, his hulking silhouette crosses the narrow room and disappears behind the door of the toilet stall. The camera frames the toilet bowl, into which three of the little paper bags fall, immediately followed by a fourth. They float on the surface for a moment and then almost immediately thereafter are carried away by the loud cascade of water as he flushes the toilet. Leaning over one of the wash basins now, the fat man washes his hands for a long time and then, taking a handkerchief out of his pocket, he dries them with slow gestures, his torso bent slightly forward, his blotched face, like that of an anatomical figure with the skin removed, a vivid pink in the mirror against the background of white tiles. Balancing on the edge of the fountain, holding to the pipe for support, several youngsters are standing on tiptoe to peek inside the barn above the frame hung with burlap sacks to hide the movie screen from view. Limited at the top by the lintel of the door and at the bottom by the upper edge of the frame, the visible area is reduced to a horizontal band approximately one-third as tall as it is wide, in which portions of objects, bodies, or faces can be seen. The sound of the jet of water falling into the basin of the fountain and the sound of the overflow, though more muted, prevent the words of the dialogue being thundered out inside the barn by the scratchy loudspeaker from being understandable. On the surface of the totally black water of the basin, constantly traversed by concentric ripples that grow larger as they move outward from the point where the jet of water falls, the yellow reflections of the electric light bulb suspended between the four walnut trees move slightly. The air, full of the dampness of the meadows and woods, is beginning to turn cool. Above the sound of the water, one can suddenly hear the mechanism of the church clock begin to whir, and almost immediately thereafter the bronze notes that slowly follow one upon the other in the calm night. The faces of the boys balancing on the edge of the fountain are stretched out toward the screen, their eyes opened wide. However (either because their attention has flagged out of frustration, or because they are tired from standing for so long in the same position and therefore take advantage of a pause in the action of the film), they stop trying to see from time to time and instead jostle each other and try to dislodge each other from their respective places. One of the smallest of them tumbles backward, dragging the two boys closest to him down with him, clutching at them as he falls, while those who have managed to hang on to the pipe burst into raucous laughter and shout jeering remarks. The other two boys immediately climb back up again, and holding on to the others, kick away the littlest one, who finally gives up and goes off, amid the hoots of the others, licking one of his hands and sniveling. For a moment he stands several yards away from the fountain, snuffling up the strings of greenish mucus hanging from his nostrils down over his upper lip, then suddenly bends down, picks up a stone, throws it more or less in the direction of the other boys, and then takes to his heels, followed by one of the boys who has jumped to the ground, but who soon halts, mutters a few threats, and comes back and climbs onto the edge of the fountain again. The little boy is now standing square in the middle of the road, some fifteen yards away from the fountain and the entrance to the barn. In a voice mingled with sobs, he too shouts insulting remarks at those who have chased him away and whose faces are again stretched out toward the narrow band of the screen visible to them. The little boy abruptly stops sobbing and runs over to the door of the barn where a group of little kids his size are gathered in a bunch, trying to look inside below the arm of one of them who is taller, with stiff hair cropped off in a ragged line across the back of his neck, shod in men's heavy high-top shoes without laces, standing barring the entrance. Either out of indulgence, or because the images succeeding each other on the screen have captured his attention, he has allowed the little boys in the first row to creep a little way past him. However, as the newcomer tries to push his way into the group, a scuffle ensues which rouses him from his attentive contemplation, provoking his wrath, whereupon he indiscriminately cuffs at them and the boys take to their heels beneath his blows, scattering in a creaking of wooden shoes and clogs, as he abandons the chase and, muttering curses, goes back to his place to stand guard once more. Amid the jeers of the group perched on the edge of the fountain, the boys wander aimlessly along the road. Giving up, two of them head off in the direction of the bridge. Others warily make their way back toward the doorway again and halt, cautiously keeping their distance from the young guard. The boy whose upper lip is covered with thick trickles of mucus hops about in one place, alternately parting his legs and bringing them together, like a jumping-jack, as he shouts defiant insults at the guard, and then, on obtaining no reaction from him, he joins another boy about his size, with whom he begins an animated discussion, commenting on the images shown in the two posters displayed above the logs piled up underneath the corn-drying poles. After a moment it is the poster showing the brick wall and the soot-colored sky that seems to monopolize their attention, and hopping up and down again in front of his pal, the little boy mimes a fight with bare fists such as the one shown in the picture on the poster where, in the distance, one of the silhouettes outlined against the pinkish hole in the clouds is falling backward above the two nearly touching heads of the bride and the young man with the sheep's face dressed in a tuxedo. The words or the onomatopoeic sounds exchanged by the young men at the top of their lungs are drowned out by the earsplitting noise from the jukebox into which the merrymakers slip one coin after another the moment that a record ends. Accompanying his gesture with the same significant sweep of his hand that includes all those present in the bar, one or the other of the young men in the party slaps a bill down on the counter, now dotted with little pools of juniper liqueur, whereupon the fat woman with a mustache immediately spirits it away, after having wiped it on her apron. Leaning on, or rather, clinging, to the counter, two of the young men are carrying on an incoherent conversation, accompanied by much gesticulation. In the center of the room, in the narrow empty area between the enameled stove and the tables, the wag is dancing all by himself, his arms bent at the elbow and spread apart, wriggling his shoulders up and down as though he were shaking an imaginary winnowing basket, snapping his fingers in time to the music, his head thrown back in an ecstatic pose, arching his back, rhythmically waggling his pelvis, and thrusting it forward in a series of obscene jerks that cause the thick tow-colored locks of hair falling over his ears to sway back and forth. Seated next to the young man who a few moments earlier has been showing signs of fatigue, hovering over him like a mother, another young man is forcing him to swallow, despite his protests, the contents of the little glasses in the form of inverted cones which the woman keeps filling one after the other and which one of the young men standing next to the counter comes over and sets down on the table. His face still bathed in the shadow cast by the visor of his cap, the man in the leather jacket is now standing all alone at the end of the counter, across which the barmaid and the bridegroom, now face to face, are exchanging a few words in low voices. Although her face still has a hostile and reserved expression, the barmaid seems to have relaxed a little. As he continues to dance and snap his fingers, the wag watches the couple out of the corner of his eye and points them out to the two young men engaged in conversation next to the bar with a slight motion of his head, accompanied by a merry wink, shouting to one and all, in time to the music We're having one last celebration We're having one last celebration! In an endless stream, the luminous bubbles glide slowly past the luxury hotels on the avenue bordered with palm trees, and one after the other the roman candles shoot up in the air and fall back in showers of sparks. The sea seems to be a milky green against the light, barely rising with the swell. Its surface resembles silk crumpled in soft folds over which there play pink reflections, forming in the sunlight a thousand dazzling-bright stars against which there are silhouetted the bodies of the bathers standing in the foam of the waves as they break on the shore, the waterbikes, the small boats rising and falling with the gentle swell, the diving platforms, the motorboats, and the water-skiers whose feet leave a trail of silver aigrettes. Indifferent to this spectacle, the fat man dressed in a dark suit walks away from the taxi he has just gotten out of and begins to climb the flight of steps in front of the entrance to the luxury hotel with the ponderous architecture and the pink cupolas, and then, changing his mind, he goes back to the sidewalk, turns to his right, and walks along the terrace where waiters in white tunics with gilt-braid epaulets are leaning down underneath the parasols of old ladies with faces covered with too much makeup and loud-colored dresses, so as to take their orders. He walks along with a heavy step in his suit appropriate for all seasons, the suit of a person to whom changing fashion is a matter of indifference, a person who is accustomed to living in air-conditioned interiors and never having to walk more than the three or four yards separating some entry, next to which there stands a doorman with stripes on his sleeves, and the edge of the sidewalk, where a chauffeur closes behind him the door of one of those cars with no grace or style, also massive and indifferent to passing fashions, with bodies that are invariably as highly polished as mirrors, and like the suits of their owners, invariably dark-colored. His ruddy Anglo-Saxon face with the impassive expression has something childish and vulnerable about it that is counterbalanced by the enigmatic gaze that filters through eyelids narrowed even more than usual in order to protect his eyes against the blinding light. As though lost in thought, he passes a newspaper stand, halts, retraces his steps, already taking a coin out of his pants pocket, and then stands there motionless, in full sunlight, his eyes glancing at the headlines as he nervously turns the pages of a newspaper. A long traveling shot follows two boys walking along, as behind them the background of foliage, of a fresh green color, dotted with black shadows and little round patches gleaming in the sunlight, glides along from right to left. Their light-skinned bodies make their way along with somewhat clumsy movements, the leg brought forward with each stride flexing noticeably in order to damp the force of the contact of their bare feet with the clods of earth or stubble, their arms half-raised, elbows outstretched, their forearms flat against the air, as though to lean on it. Once they have reached the end of the wall of vegetation forming the boundary of the cornfield, they pause for a moment, their torsos leaning forward, spying all around them, and then, taking off again, they descend a slope, cross a meadow, and reach the bushes bordering the river, just before the bend where the curtain of poplars rises in the air. Having arrived at that particular spot, they remain hidden there, crouching side by side, panting again, casting quick glances all about, at times in the direction of the waterfall, at times toward the first houses of the hamlet whose tall violet-colored roofs appear above the orchards. The furious buzzing of the wings of the dying fly, stuck fast among the others on the strip of sticky paper, is interrupted by longer and longer silences, during which one hears only the monotonous tick-tock of the pendulum of the clock. On the kitchen table, not far from the long oval platter with the rabbit lying on it, there is now a wicker basket three-quarters full of freshly picked mushrooms. The wicker has taken on a gray patina. The twisted handle is strengthened by a piece of string, also gray, that has been carefully wound around it. The mushrooms give off a faint odor of underbrush, humus, and wet earth. They are of two varieties. The larger ones are yellow, with lengthwise folds along the stem that spread out to form an annulus, like the bell of a trumpet with turned-up edges. The smaller ones have thick white stems surmounted by a round cap of a brownish-violet color. Bits of black dirt, moss, or pine needles, in the case of the smaller ones, are still stuck to their stems. In order, doubtless, to protect it from flies, someone has thrown a clean cloth over the body of the rabbit. The ends of its paws with their little fur boots and the head with a single eye are the only parts of its body protruding beyond the cloth. Despite the folds still pressed into the stiff material, one can make out beneath the cloth the form of the skinned body, the two parted thighs, the concave belly, and the narrow rib cage. Someone has turned out the electric light bulb that was swinging back and forth above the table. In the semidarkness enveloping more and more of the kitchen, and in contrast with the white cloth, the bloody flesh of the head is so dark a red that it is almost black. A little pool of blood has gradually formed on the oilcloth, below the empty eye socket. The lowered blinds allow only a dim light to filter through them, plunging the entire room into that warm half-shadow such as that in sickrooms, where one walks on tiptoe and speaks only in a soft voice. The angle of the slats of the blinds lets in only those rays of light reflected by the white-hot surface of the highway, which are directed upward, projecting on the ceiling moving shadows that turn round and round like the blades of a ventilating fan. Beneath the sheet pulled up breast-high, one can make out the form of the body lying spread-legged on the bed, the parted thighs, the faint swelling of the pubis, the flat belly, and the twin mounds of the breasts. By contrast with the snow-white sheet, the face without makeup (or perhaps with too much makeup) seems congested, of too pronounced a pink, tending toward a violet tint in the half-light. A bottle of mineral water, a glass, and a tube of pills are sitting on the little table next to the head of the bed. With the exception of the chest, which rises and falls regularly, the body is motionless. The eyes are open, staring emptily at the ceiling. The heavy-set man in the dark suit enters the next room, carefully closes the door behind him, walks over to the door leading to the adjoining bedroom, and stands at the threshold for a moment, contemplating the body sprawled out on the bed. The woman has not turned her head. After a moment the man says Were you asleep? The woman's only reply is to turn her head and stare at him. He says Everything is all right he's going to be released some time this evening. The woman appears not to understand and continues to stare at him. He draws closer then with his heavy tread and says Don't take too many of those pills they . . . , but doesn't finish his sentence, the woman's arm suddenly emerging from the sheets, her hand darting past his and coming down violently on top of the little tube. He then wearily shrugs his shoulders and says Did you hear what I said? He's going to be released in a little while: lack of evidence. The woman's eyes continue to stare at him for a moment, then her head returns to its initial position and she says slowly, as though she were addressing the ceiling, and in a flat voice that seems to have difficulty articulating the words Bunch of riff-raff. The man shrugs his shoulders again, starts to turn away, halts midway, and says, leaning his head to one side in the direction of the woman Don't you want me to have something to eat sent up, you ought to . . . , and then his voice dies away for a second time. He stands there in that position for a few seconds, contemplating the motionless face, his own features set in an indescribable expression of suffering and fatigue, and then turns his back and lumbers off into the other room. Shortly thereafter one hears the wooden frame of an armchair creak and the sound of the pages of a newspaper being turned. The icy water of the river comes up to the two boys' chests as they cross it at right angles to the current, which is quite rapid at this spot, using their outstretched arms as a counterweight to keep their balance, their shoulders pivoting slightly at each step, first to one side and then to the other, cautiously feeling their way across the uneven stones on the bottom, slipping from time to time and struggling to regain their equilibrium, one arm striking the water. Their torsos seem to float on the surface, cut off a little below the nipples, though prolonged below it by their bellies and by their legs telescoped by the refraction of the water, looking wavy and white against the bottom of moss-covered stones. Once they have reached the opposite shore, they hoist themselves up onto the bank by clinging to the low branches of a bush, their dripping wet skin again dotted with goose flesh. The second boy has not yet stood completely upright when all of a sudden his companion gives a start and quickly leaps backward, their two bodies bumping into each other, and then, half locked in embrace and off-balance, crawling clumsily sideways like a sort of four-footed beast, their legs becoming entangled, their eyes staring in terror at something black and shiny rising up in the grass along the bank where they have been the moment before, the flat head turned at a right angle in their direction, one of the two boys bending down, his hand searching at his feet for a clod of earth which he throws in a fury, shouting You filthy thing!, and then a strip of burnished steel stretching out, weaving back and forth, and then the next moment, like a dark gray stick emerging obliquely from the river, the head now bent at an obtuse angle, the rigid stick cleaving the water, leaving behind it a silvery V traced across the dark reflections of the trees, proceeding in short little zigzag strokes, first to one side and then to the other, the surface of the water behind it agitated by sinuous little eddies, and then reaching the opposite shore and disappearing, the two boys still petrified, still panting a little, mechanically lying there leaning against each other, the first boy saying Geez, I almost stepped right on top of it The disgusting thing! Did you see it?, hurling another clod of earth across the river at the spot where the snake has disappeared, repeating Geez I almost . . . Geez! The disgusting thing! Geez!, the two of them lying there, their hearts pounding, too frightened even to shiver, the bigger boy finally moving, saying Talk about your vipers! I've never seen such a . . . , and the other That wasn't a viper, vipers don't swim, and the first one Not a viper! geez you saw its head didn't you? and the other It was a grass snake, and the first one A grass snake? Geez haven't you ever seen a viper? All you had to do was look at its head Geez!, both of them continuing to argue as they start walking again, keeping close to the bushes, watching carefully where they put their feet down, the first one repeating Geez, I almost stepped right on top of it geez!, the sibilant sound of the waterfall, mingled with the shrill calls of the youngsters, closer and closer now, until finally they are again able to see the basin, the green water along the edges, then blue, and then almost black, and the luminous bodies moving about in the sunlight. The two boys fall motionless then, hiding three-quarters of their bodies behind a bush, carefully scrutinizing the basin, the waterfall, and the clumps of bushes at the top of it, outlined against the sky where the clouds are still gliding peacefully along. After a moment one of the boys nudges the other with his elbow, and without ceasing to keep an eye on the top of the waterfall, they both run over to a pile of clothes lying at the edge of the water, which they pick up, along with two fishing poles, and paying no attention to the shouts from the other boys, their clothes rolled up in a ball under one arm, their shoes dangling from the end of two fingers, and their fishing poles held horizontally in the other hand, they walk off downstream along the riverbank. Although the jukebox continues to fill the bar with its booming, deafening din, the gleeful young groomsmen have become less boisterous and the sound level has decreased somewhat. The wag has stopped wriggling his hips in time to the music and has joined the two young men who are leaning on the counter talking together. From time to time he raises his voice again as with the flat of his hand he pushes away the boy standing facing him, who also raises his voice, the two of them shouting vague remarks at each other which might be either challenges, categorical statements, or repeated denials, and then their voices drop again. One of the young men sitting on the banquette is now lolling backward, his parted legs stretched out underneath the table, staring straight ahead, looking sick, and his companion, losing interest in him, is listening to the incoherent conversation among the three others. The man in the leather jacket is still leaning on his elbows at the very end of the bar, not saying a word, his face still hidden by the shadow of his visor, and seemingly deaf to the words that the fat woman leaning over toward him is murmuring to him. Without stopping talking and almost mechanically, the wag fishes another bill out of his pocket and slaps it down on the bar, shouting over his shoulder Come on everybody, one last round! The barmaid, who has been leaning over the counter talking in a low voice with the young bridegroom, suddenly stands upright, says a few words in the ear of the fat woman who has already started to fill the glasses again, and passing close by the man in the leather jacket without looking at him, disappears through a little door situated behind the bar counter into a room where one catches a brief glimpse of an enameled stove, the corner of a table covered with oilcloth, and a sideboard painted brown. The wag, who has observed this little scene, goes over to the jukebox and slips another coin in it, setting off another earsplitting burst of sound, and then walks over to the end of the counter where the man in the leather jacket is standing leaning on his elbows, making cordial gestures and speaking to him in a deliberately loud tone of voice so as to be heard over all the noise, as the young bridegroom, walking unsteadily, furtively makes his way over to the outside door of the bar and disappears. In the kitchen the barmaid quickly throws a beige coat over her shoulders and opens the door that leads to a rear courtyard. In the light projected outside one can see the silvery glint of the fine rain against the black background of the dark night. Frowning, the girl lifts her face up toward the dark sky, then comes out, closing the door behind her. Hidden behind a bush, the two boys hastily put their shirts and their short pants back on over their wet bodies, still casting wary glances in the direction of the top of the waterfall. Once they are dressed again, they quickly unwind their fishlines and sit down in the grass to bait their hooks with the worms that one of them removes from an old medicine tin. The little worms smeared with mud twist and turn in the boys' fingers, which they then wipe on their pants. As soon as the hooks are baited, they hide their soaking-wet bathing trunks in a thicket and cast their lines into the river, as far upstream as possible. The corks float downstream with the current, pass in front of them, move farther along, and then, having been abruptly jerked upstream again, are once again carried downstream by the current. The boys seem to be paying little attention to their fishing, still casting wary glances from time to time in the direction of the top of the waterfall, and then, as time passes, gradually regaining their self-assurance. The water is so clear that one can see the white blobs of the worms also drifting downstream with the current, occasionally bumping against a stone on the bottom, floating around it, and being carried off downstream again. After a moment one of the boys takes a crumpled package of cigarettes out of his pocket and the two of them lean their heads toward each other above the match that the one boy has struck. The puffs of smoke that they try to disperse by waving one hand in the air rise in little blue clouds in the sunlight. Despite the watchful glances that they continue to cast all about them, they give a start on hearing a noise very close by and see a young woman who has stopped several yards away from them, holding a little girl by the hand. The young woman says What do you expect to catch here this isn't the right place to . . . She is wearing a blouse in a mauve and white print, a brown skirt, black stockings, and black cotton sandals with rope soles. She is waving a branch of a walnut tree in order to keep the horseflies away from the little girl, who is clutching a bouquet of field flowers in her free hand. The young woman suddenly bursts out laughing and says Don't bother putting out your cigarettes I won't tell on you Good Lord you certainly are stupid, you two! The smaller boy says We know what we're doing There was one that was just about to bite But now you've naturally scared it away That sure was clever of you. His foot nervously crushes the cigarette in the grass, but it stubbornly continues to smolder. Pulling with all her strength on the hand clasping her wrist, the little girl reaches the bank of the river and leans out over the water. She says I want to see it where is it? One of the boys says in a furious tone of voice It's darted away under that big rock If you keep on making such a racket we won't even see the tail of another one! The servant girl says for the second time Nobody's ever caught any fish in this spot don't you realize they can see you from here? The little girl pulls even harder and bends down to gather a yellow flower growing along the bank, almost over-hanging the water. One of the boys says Stop making all that racket and clear out of here! In places the rays of sunlight pierc-ing the foliage turn the moss on the stones at the bottom of the river a golden yellow. The shadow of the south slope of the valley has nearly reached the opposite bank. As it begins to set, the sun brightens the colors of the circus posters on the wall of the barn. Unlike the faces of the man in the royal blue swallow-tail coat and those of the ring attendants, which now have a fearful expression on them at the sight of the revolvers, that of the clown beneath his makeup remains frozen, once and for all, whatever his gestures or words, in a dumb show of outrage and stupefaction. The lips of the enormous mouth extending over his cheeks and down his chin look like fat sausages, and with their drooping corners they are reminiscent of the mouths of those masks behind which actors in the tragedies of antiquity con-cealed their features. The bizarre onomatopoeic sounds escaping from it, reminiscent of an animal cry, also contribute to this impression of dehumanization, being seemingly emitted by some robot with a limited vocabulary and a limited number of gestures, a crude, simplified prototype intended to be the object of violence, indignation, and howls of derisive laughter. Preceded by his two divergent shadows, running along in a grotesque manner, stumbling and tripping, the clown chases the man in tails and the ring attendants, shooting off his revolvers and shouting furious invectives at them as they flee as fast as their legs can carry them. Even after they have disappeared behind the red curtains, he continues to walk in their direction, thrusts his head through the slit between the curtains, his buttocks in the outsize pair of pants jerking in wrath, thus sending the audience into howls of laughter, and then, swaying back and forth like a tenpin, he returns to the center of the ring, where he halts dead in his tracks. The smoke from the cap pistol shots hovers in the air in a bluish wisp suspended in the beams from the spotlights. The clown then emits his bizarre cry, which is immediately answered by the barking noise from the gaping vamp of his shoe. The bursts of laughter that have been heard from the benches around the ring during the chase scene ring out once again. The old woman pushing her wicker baby buggy with the scythe lying diagonally across the grass that she has cut has long since disappeared behind the trees in the orchards. The shadow of the slope has also long since crossed the river, invaded the meadow, and crossed the road leading to the sawmill, and it is now mounting the opposite slope, enveloping the barn. It has even gone beyond the edge of the woods and is beginning to ascend the tall rock cliff which rises straight up, towering over the slope covered with fallen earth in which scraggly little bushes are growing. The tigers are leaping all around the shocks of tousled, but now dry, hair of the two boys, who have placed their heads one just above the other so that each of them may glue one eye to the tear in the poster. The man is lying on his back, with an old army overcoat spread out underneath the woman to protect them from contact with the floor of beaten earth dotted with oil stains and strewn with little bits of fodder. The woman's torso is almost perpendicular to the man's: lying on her side, with one shoulder resting in the hollow of the man's waist and her head at the level of his belly covered with dark hairs, she has bent back her legs, still sheathed in black cotton stockings rolled like a sausage around the middle of her thighs, apart from which she is stark naked, her mauve and white printed blouse, her brassiere, and her brown skirt hanging from the handle of a plow leaning against the muddy tractor painted orange. Her backside is thrust out toward the spectators, so that one can see the slit of her vulva peeking out between the hairy lips, at the point where her buttocks and thighs meet. Still holding the man's stiff member by the base with one hand, she sucks the end of it for a long time, occasionally thrusting it deep inside her mouth, her lips then almost touching her hand, her head slowly moving up and down, her cheeks forming hollows as she sucks. The rectangular surface of the screen is now divided into nearly square compartments, three crosswise and two and a half lengthwise. Each compartment is provided with a door framed in unpainted wood, weathered to a gray color, on which one's eye can follow the striations of the lighter veins standing out in slight relief. The doors are kept closed by means of a rudimentary latch, a simple bit of wood pivoting on a screw and held shut by a catch consisting of a large rusty nail hammered into a curve. The crude frames are covered with chicken wire with wide hexagonal meshes behind which one can see the shapes of rabbits. The doors, hung more or less out of true, sag at the edge opposite their hinges. Two bony hands with earth-colored skin blotched with freckles suddenly appear on the left of the screen. The gray fingernails curve down like claws over the blunt fingertips. Huge veins of a blue tending toward green snake along in relief and form knots like roots beneath the skin. As the left hand turns the latch of each frame and opens the door, the right hand sticks several handfuls of fresh-cut grass into each box. The far end of these cell-like compartments is dark, so that, depending on their position inside them, the round shapes of the rabbits at times appear to be bathed in shadow and indistinguishable from it, roughly indicated by a paintbrush which has merely placed a few highlights here and there, and at times in chiaroscuro, their blurred contours sinking into the bituminous wash, or else, when the rabbits stand close to the chicken wire, appearing in sharp outline with their colors heightened by the contrast with the dark background. Frightened by the doors being opened, they hop jerkily about. The majority of them have fur of a delicate gray color, with white spots. Their eyes are yellow or chestnut brown. Their silky hairs become sparser inside their long ears, the pink skin of which is visible, and around their lips, which are also pink. Their muzzles quiver rapidly and continuously. Now and again the woman raises her head and her lips that have been pressed tightly around the cylindrical shaft of the member, and then around the glans, allow the latter to appear, swollen and hard, bright pink in color, gleaming with saliva. A long silvery thread connects it to the half-open mouth and then breaks when, throwing her head still farther back, the girl contemplates for a moment the outstretched budlet, her hand moving upward and pulling the foreskin down, covering and uncovering the glans with a motion at times brisk and at times languid, as she watches it swell still more, and then, pulling the prepuce down below the violet-colored rim of the glans, she suddenly lowers her head and swallows it, her cheeks again forming hollows, her eyes closed, as a muffled sound escapes the man's lips. Little round bits of carrots, reddish-orange in color with a pale green center, along with other vegetable debris and dark brown pellets of dung, are strewn over the floor of the cell-like cages. At the very back of one of the cages little young rabbits are huddled one against the other, half hidden by their mother's plump body. The bony, mummy-like hands are spattered with sticky little lumps, of a dark yellow color, made up of crumbled and moistened crusts of bread, like the feed one gives to chickens, which have stuck to the fingers. When she bends over to open the doors of the cages farthest away, on the right of the screen, the profile of the old woman with the dog's jaw appears on the left, the skin criss-crossed by an unbelievable number of deep wrinkles, the chin abnormally close to the upper jaw, the lips drawn inside the mouth, the absence of teeth causing the cheeks to form hollows, as though she were sucking on something. Between the red-rimmed, flaccid eyelids, the eyes are of a faded blue, covered with a sort of whitish cloud. The locks of the girl's hair hang down vertically, hiding three-quarters of her face. Little by little, through a series of movements of his shoulders and back which cause his torso to creep sideways, the man shifts position so that his hand that has been stroking the girl's hair and shoulders descends to her lower back and then to her buttocks, caressing first one of them and then the other, and then one finger follows the cleft leading downward and slips between them, brushing past the anus, descending farther still, reaching the vulva and parting the lips of it, and then mounting up to the invisible clitoris, over which it rubs back and forth. One can see the red hand with the strong bones and the folds encrusted with grease move almost imperceptibly for a moment, and then plunge down farther still as the finger penetrates deep inside the vagina, the hand resuming its slow movement, the woman's head moving up and down faster and faster, the dangling locks of her tousled hair swaying back and forth, in the same rhythm, a muffled sound emerging from her throat, the two movements, that of the hand buried between her thighs and that of the head beneath its cap of long swaying locks, accelerating until the woman's legs suddenly lash out and she lies there, stiff and tense, her thighs joined and jerking faintly, clasping between them the hand that is now motionless, the inarticulate sounds forced from their two throats mingling, then ceasing, the two bodies now motionless, the woman's head having fallen flat on the man's belly, her hand still tightly clasped around the base of the man's erect member with the congested, sticky glans. Despite her expressionless eyes, the hands of the woman whose dog's profile is outlined against the rabbit hutch continue to feel about clumsily in order to open the doors of the cages, stick handfuls of grass into them, and close them again. Inside the first cages that she has attended to, several rabbits have gradually moved closer to the fresh food and are beginning to nibble hungrily at it. With terrified little hops they immediately return to the backs of their cages where they huddle in a ball, their ears pinned back, when the hands open one of the doors again, fumble about inside, remove one of the rabbits, and examine it by feeling it. The old woman repeats this operation in three of the cages, replacing the animal each time and closing the door with the rudimentary latch again. Finally she removes a fourth rabbit, and the camera slowly moves closer as the woman straightens up, lifting the rabbit up in the air at the same time, outlined now above the hutch, whereupon the camera stops moving, framing, on the left, the profile slashed with wrinkles, over the forehead of which, escaping the confines of the hat that looks exactly the same as always, there hang down locks of white hair, and on the right, the rabbit held firmly by the ears. In its terror, its long silky mustache has curved inward and is lying against the two sides of its muzzle with the soft little hairs. Its hind legs bent halfway back lash out convulsively in the empty air. Its body hanging by the ears sways feebly back and forth, its back wriggling and jerking helplessly.

Giving advance warning from afar of their approach, in the form of a shrill chorus of honking horns, a procession of a dozen or so automobiles makes its way through the dense traffic flowing between the rows of squat buildings, faced with brick or covered with a dark coat of plaster, lining each side of the paved highway where heavily laden trucks, semi-trailers, and dump trucks are jouncing along amid a clatter of metal, together with a steady stream of other conveyances, the majority of them also commercial vehicles. The cars in the procession are almost all small, low-powered ones, and their occupants crowded together in the narrow bodies resemble giants crammed into ridiculously tiny toy cars, carefully polished and decorated with tulle ribbons tied to their door handles and the ends of their radio antennas. Their drivers, almost all of them young men, are having a sort of race or gymkhana between themselves, recklessly passing the heavy vehicles, tucking back in the stream of traffic, and pulling out again with repeated honks of their horns, leaning their faces, with expressions at once gleeful and fiercely competitive, out the doors. As they pass by, one catches a glimpse of older people sitting in the back seats, dressed in their Sunday best, the women wearing hats and gloves and bright silk dresses and the men's mouths set in frozen smiles. The low gray sky is diffusing that sort of timeless light that toward the end of autumn seems to hover in the air with no noticeable change from the half-light of dawn to that of twilight, with the same fixity as artificial lighting that is sufficient but quite dim, and falling with the same unvarying intensity on the background consisting of a jumble of buildings where there follow, one after the other, long blind walls of factories or warehouses, broken glass roofs, houses, buildings several stories high or low façades with windows hung with grayish curtains between which there sometimes appears, immediately next to the glass, some sort of potted plant with leaves the same shade of gray. Her attention attracted by the noise, a young woman opens the door of a cheap bar located on the ground floor of a house that is indistinguishable from the others adjoining it, which are also faced in brick, save for a simple sign hung perpendicular to the wall, in the form of a red plastic disk that doubtless glows in the dark, on which one can see, in white letters, the name of a brand of beer. A row of bottles with different labels are set out on a wooden shelf that runs across the inside of the upper part of the window, the panes of which are decorated with bright-colored posters advertising brands of apéritifs or juniper liqueurs. The bricks of the façade are of a pinkish earth color, though they have turned a sooty black below the window sills, where the rain never reaches them to wash them clean. The young woman with a little too much makeup on her face and a new permanent wave a bit too carefully groomed is wearing a shiny pink silk blouse, a black skirt, and dark brown stockings, which are also shiny. With her head turned toward the right, she is watching the gates of the railway crossing go down, barring the tracks that cut across the long suburban street some fifty yards beyond the bar. The loud buzz of the warning bell sounds as the metal arms with red and white stripes painted on them come down. Hanging from them is a fringe of metal rods that gradually stretch out to form a curtain underneath the arms, which finally fall motionless in a horizontal position after having bounced slightly on their supports. Driven with a daring hand at the wheel, the first car in the procession has managed to pass through the crossing, just a few seconds before the bars have come down, and stops shortly thereafter in order to wait for the other cars following, which are being held up on the other side. In front of the car that has stopped, the right side of the highway is now deserted, whereas a long line of vehicles stretches out in the opposite direction, waiting for the crossing gates to open again. The first vehicle in line is a truck-and-trailer loaded with long rust-colored rods that stick out at the rear, bending beneath their own weight. Attached to the end of the longest one are a frayed red rag and a lantern. The dangling ends of the rods, which create an empty space between the rear of the trailer and the following vehicles, are so situated that if a dotted line were drawn diagonally across the highway, the threshold of the bar and the stopped car would both fall along it, so that as a result the occupants of the car see the red rag and the lantern sway back and forth below the door where the young woman in the pink blouse is standing. Inside this car, doubtless a rented one, which is luxurious by comparison with the other modest compact cars in the procession and which also has more decorations, being adorned with two large tulle ribbons stretched out in a V over the hood, the barmaid in turn can make out a young man wearing a tuxedo and the bride wreathed in her wedding veil, the two of them sitting far apart on the back seat. Forced to a halt by the barrier and having nothing better to do, the drivers in the wedding procession while away the time by honking their horns, which answer each other insistently, stridently, on discordant notes and at different cadences. The buttonhole in the lapel of the young man's tuxedo is decorated with a white carnation. Beneath his curly pale blond hair, his face between the long sideburns that look like tow is vaguely reminiscent of that of a sheep. The bride's face is of that impersonal and interchangeable type that seems destined, so to speak, to be framed by the ritual background of white bridal veils and orange blossoms piled up in rented cars. Nonchalantly leaning his elbow on the door and jolted by the vibrations of the huge idling motor that are making the sheet metal of the hood quiver, the driver of the truck-and-trailer sitting high up in his cab looks down indifferently at the little porcelain mask wreathed in tulle which the drivers of the other stopped vehicles are also looking at, for want of anything better to do. The warning bell at the crossing continues to ring loudly. Men and women cross the tracks on foot in one direction or the other, pushing their motorbikes or their bicycles alongside them, and one can also hear the regular clanging of the little iron gate for pedestrians slamming shut behind them. The face of the young woman standing on the threshold of the bar is devoid of all expression. Alongside and a little to the rear of her the fleshy face of a woman whose upper lip is adorned with a mustache of black hairs is now also framed in the doorway. The driver of the car in which the bride and groom are sitting continues to honk his horn uninterruptedly, leaning out the door and looking at the other cars blocked on the other side of the crossing, the drivers of which answer his gleeful shouts. One can see the newlyweds smilingly exchanging a few words, a bit embarrassed at being the object of the glances of the occupants of the cars stopped at the crossing. The young man does not appear to notice the open door of the bar and the girl in the pink blouse to whom the fat woman says a few words, whereupon the two of them go back inside and the door closes again. Preceded by the regular sound of puffs of steam, a tall locomotive approaches the crossing, slowly picking up speed. Black and majestic with its oiled piston rods, its huge wheels of gleaming metal, it passes by, shaking the ground with dull thuds, as though propelled by the grayish cloud streaming out from between its wheels, and draws away, its awesome panting gradually replaced by the monotonous sound of the coal cars painted a reddish earth color, with sloping sides like enormous coffins, rolling by one after the other, also causing the earth to tremble as their wheels pass over the rail joints. The young bridegroom casts a quick glance in the direction of the closed door of the bar, then turns and looks again, with a smile, at the anonymous face in the white veil alongside him. Although it is not raining, the paving stones, the walls, the tall brick chimneys, and even the puffs of smoke escaping from them seem wet, as though every object, including the impalpable, almost flat spirals, were attracting and absorbing invisible droplets in suspension in the gray air, reminding one of those watercolors in dull hues in which the sky, the surface of the canals, the trees with black branches, the stones appear to be made of one and the same substance diluted by water. The last iron coal car with reddish sides disappears on the left, like a curtain being drawn aside, revealing the remainder of the procession of cars whose drivers begin to honk their horns even louder. A few moments go by before the double barrier slowly rises, and without even waiting for the metal arms to return to their absolutely vertical position, the second car in the procession leaps forward, cutting off a light truck, and begins chasing after the newlyweds' car, which is already rushing off at top speed, also honking uninterruptedly, along the side of the highway free of cars. The iron grille of the movie theater, which is separated from the bar by a narrow alleyway, is closed. The herd of red cows has disappeared. After having eliminated a certain number of the bits of film that they have looked through (among them an automobile race, a scene from a western, and another in period costumes), the two boys sitting in the grass under the apple tree have finally set aside five which seem to them to have a certain unity and which they are now endeavoring to place in an order that they are still uncertain is the right one, arguing among themselves, and looking them over several times more. Every so often the bigger of the two mechanically raises to his mouth the finger with the broken nail that he holds to one side as he grabs one of the little strips of film with his other fingers and examines it for a moment before laying it down again. To the first three (that is to say: 1) the one in which the heavy-set man can be seen sitting on a banquette next to the character with the bird's profile; 2) the same man dressed in black, standing with his head turned to one side, as though he were trying to hear what is happening in the next room, on the other side of a door whose handle he is holding in one hand; 3) the naked actress sprawled out on the bed with the rumpled sheets, with a crumpled newspaper lying on the rug next to the bed), there have been added a fourth and a fifth which the bigger boy has taken out of his pocket later, each of them consisting of five frames, in which one can follow the various phases of a single scene, though it is obvious that between the two series an intermediate phase is missing. Unlike the images that can be seen in the first fragments, this episode seems to be one with a great deal of violent action, at least on the part of its main character, a young man dressed in blue jeans, his face contorted with anger, standing approximately in the center of the scene, his legs apart, his arms flailing the air from left to right so rapidly that they leave on each of the images on the film only a vague trace, and in the last image are frozen motionless at the end of their travel, thrust out sideways, while at the same time there extends from his open hands a sort of nebulous white trail suspended in the air, which the woman (dressed now in one of those negligees that only actresses wear, in shiny silk edged in swan's-down) is watching fan out, panic-stricken, her right hand raised up to her mouth as though to stifle a scream, her left arm lowered, just behind her, searching about for something to lean on for support, her body slightly tilted, as though drawing backward, with one leg that is bent at the knee and the other, thrust forward, emerging almost entirely from her magnificent negligee. The décor is that of one of those rooms with costly, stereotyped furnishings such as in those films in which the protagonists, apparently freed of all financial constraints, move indifferently among pieces of furniture that are luxurious but stuffy: outsize divans, marble tables, and Ming vases transformed into lamp stands with shades in the form of pagodas, or filled with giant bouquets changed each morning by a florist with whom a standing order has been placed. However, despite the sumptuous nature of the furniture (or perhaps because of it), the arrangement and maintenance of which presuppose the services of a paid staff of employees, the entire décor leaves one with an impression of emptiness, impersonality, and desolation, as though the protagonists were merely passing through, staying for only a short time in a temporary and artificial ambiance that has nothing to do with them, set up the day before by stagehands standing ready to take it down and isolated from the rest of the world by floodlights, like a minuscule and ephemeral little island of light in the vast emptiness of the cosmos, or, more simply, that of a vast movie studio, equally black and equally empty. Without letting go of the end of the strip of film that he is holding up to the sky, one of the boys lies down on his back, and turning over on his side, stretches out his free hand, twisting his neck around, to pick up one of the apples forming a circle in the grass around the foot of the tree whose branches bend down beneath the weight of the fruit. Raising his torso up, he mechanically brings the apple closer to his mouth but does not complete the gesture, doubtless pondering some detail or other in the strip, laying the apple down in the grass alongside him, taking the magnifying glass out of his comrade's hands and attentively examining the bit of film again. It is night, and the light coming from the Chinese lampshade illuminates most clearly the woman and the young man in blue jeans standing in the foreground, whereas it leaves in shadow, at the far end of the room, a heavy-set man, dressed in a dark suit, sitting on, or rather, buried in one of the deep divans. It is therefore difficult to identify with any degree of certainty on the minuscule image, even with the aid of the magnifying glass, the face of the actor, as it is also difficult to identify the actress, standing there in her negligee edged in swan's-down, and the one who, in the other bit of film, appears only lying down, her head thrown back on the pillow and her face consequently visible only upside down. The pose of the character dressed in a dark suit, who apparently is participating in the scene only as a mute witness, nonetheless recalls (arms spread out to support himself, his two hands resting flat on the seat cushions) the episode in the bar, and his general appearance, his obesity, his taciturn immobility, incline one to believe that it is indeed the same actor, although there is no way of being absolutely certain. The boy picks up the apple again, turning it around in his hand and examining it suspiciously. The shining skin, part red and part green, has a light brown disk-shaped spot in it, forming a slight dent. Making up his mind, the boy takes a big bite out of the hard flesh, on the side opposite the spot, begins chewing, and almost immediately spews out half-chewed bits of a greenish white, noisily blowing to remove the ones that have remained stuck to his lips, saying Geez, how disgusting! and angrily tossing away the fruit he has started eating, his teethmarks remaining imprinted in it. He spews out a few more bits, wipes his lips with the back of this hand, and then, picking up the little strips of film again, he holds them up to the light one after the other until he finds fragment number one again, examining it once more for some time, frowning, the two boys then reviewing, for the tenth time perhaps, the five fragments which they hand back and forth, discussing them again, handling them carefully, holding them by the edges between their thumbs and their index fingers, blowing on them from time to time to chase away an insect, and changing yet again the order in which they lay them out on the grass between the two of them. Finally, however, they agree that the sequence should start with the five images in which one can see the actress lying naked on the bed with the crumpled newspaper lying alongside it, and next the scene with the two men in the bar, and then the two fragments showing the angry young man. They are still uncertain, however, as to where to place the fragment in which one sees the man in the dark suit standing with one hand on the door handle, which in fact might be placed almost anywhere, either before or after the other scenes, though definitely not between the two shots showing the young man, which doubtless follow each other in close succession, since in the second one (taken from another angle but in the same room and with the same lighting), the woman is shown very close up in the foreground, photographed almost directly from the back, a vague whitish pile spreading out at her feet on the carpet, the man in black still motionless on the divan in the background, the young man with the sheep's head now standing next to the outside door that he has just thrown open, his legs and pelvis already turned toward the corridor, his body twisting backward, his torso pivoting around in the direction of the woman one last time, his face still contorted with anger, his mouth wide open as though he were about to shout out one last insult, one last curse, one last farewell before stepping across the threshold and slamming the door behind him, as if he were capable only of violent, uncontrolled actions: shouting, flailing his arms about, or throwing the notebooks and texts which by looking through the magnifying glass one can make out in the nebula that stretches outward, sailing through the air from his hands, one of which is still grasping the end of the book strap that was holding them together, the strap itself wriggling like a serpent above the pages and the covers of the notebooks and texts (reminiscent of those sorts of fleeting accordions that professional card sharps or conjurers stretch out between their two hands with a crackling sound of the deck of cards skillfully fanned out and then brought back together in a lightning-quick motion), the same texts and notebooks, some open, others closed, scattered every which way on the carpet at the feet of the horror-stricken woman toward whom the camera has moved closer for the last image. Sitting astride a huge motorcycle, a man dressed in a loose-fitting jacket and pants of blue cotton duck that have been mended and discolored along the seams from many washings is rolling slowly along the little road leading from the hamlet to the sawmill, inspecting the landscape around him, the fields, and on his right, the bushes and the clumps of trees along the edge of the river. His thick black hair curls over his ears in tufts and a few frizzy locks fall down over his forehead. His face is of the Mediterranean type, with a mat complexion. The folds of the skin at the joints of his fingers and on the sides of his palms are encrusted with that black, indelible stain left by oil and grease on the hands of mechanics or tractor drivers. He is wearing black rubber boots that come up almost to his knees, repaired with brick-red inner tube patches. The motorcycle slows down more and more, tracing gentle curves on the road, until it stops altogether, its rider remaining seated on the saddle, his two feet now resting on the ground, his legs supporting him, rummaging through his pockets, taking out a package of cigarettes and lighting one of them, which remains stuck between his lips, the puffs of blue smoke rising in the sunlight, as he sits there, his torso erect, continuing to survey the countryside attentively. Finally he catches sight of the group formed at the edge of the river by the two boys, the servant girl, and the little girl, and the look in his eyes becomes more penetrating. The boys' shirts, the servant girl's blouse, and the little girl's dress form clear patches against the foliage. Drawing without haste on his cigarette that he is now holding between his blackened fingers, the motorcyclist remains motionless, his eyes still turned toward the group standing on the riverbank, the motor continuing to idle, little transparent puffs of smoke, also bluish, coming out of the exhaust pipe. Too far away to make out the expression on their faces and hear the words that they are exchanging, he observes the gestures of the young servant girl in the mauve and white blouse. Although she gives no sign of having noticed his presence, she kneels down next to the little girl, and with her head at the same level as the little girl's face, says something to her, pointing several times at the two boys, one of whom finally shrugs his shoulders, and then, with a circular gesture, she points to the meadow behind them, far away from the river's edge, and the little girl obediently heads toward it, bending down from time to time to pick a flower, as the servant girl strides swiftly off downstream, toward the hamlet. The leaves of the curtain of poplars with the sunlight streaming through them stand out in yellow against the wooded background of the southern slope of the valley, engulfed in shadow. The leaves tremble slightly. The motorcyclist then races his engine and the machine takes off, rolling slowly, in the direction of the sawmill, turns with a jolt into the sunken path to the left, and disappears behind the bushes on the slope. The clump of hazelnut trees standing by themselves a short distance away from the edge of the woods conceals the lower part of the wall of the barn on which the circus posters are pasted. In the blinding glare of the spotlights, a fantastic-looking performer advances toward the clown in the grotesque costume, causing an amazed murmur to run along the benches. This apparition is wearing delicate white ballet slippers, the calves of its legs are sheathed in white stockings, its one-piece costume with bouffant pants and a top that clings to its torso is made of white silk, and its face covered with a layer of white grease paint is surmounted by a white felt cap, in the form of a cone, tilted over one ear. At each of its movements, the spangles of its costume, its powdered hand loaded down with rings, and even its eyelids, covered with brilliant jade-colored makeup, give off iridescent sparkles like those of precious stones such as topazes, rubies, and amethysts. A great golden sun surrounded with tongues of flame and a silver moon are embroidered on the front and back of its tight-fitting top sprinkled with stars that blaze in the light, gleaming as brightly as its eyes of an indefinable color which also looks metallic, their sparkle enhanced by the rapid fluttering of the creature's eyelids. Unreal and immaculate, it stands out against the benches and the rows of spectators sitting in the half-shadow as though against an ink-black background. The pale narrow face has only two spots of color on it, the thin-lipped mouth, touched up with red, and an eyebrow carefully painted on in deep black, in the form of a tilted comma with the pointed end jutting upward. The servant girl has disappeared behind the trees in the orchards. The little girl has sat down in the grass behind the two boys, who have started fishing again, apparently almost as half-heartedly as a short while before, the focus of their preoccupation having shifted, however, for now it is not the waterfall that the bigger one is watching attentively, indifferent to the bob on his fish line, but instead the orchards at the edge of the hamlet. He nonetheless turns around once or twice, trying to catch a glimpse of the motorcycle, but it has now disappeared. Three little girls about twelve years old appear downstream, leaving the village and walking up the river along the bank, bending down every so often to pick a flower and chattering among themselves. Two of them are wearing checked pinafores and are bare-legged. The spindly legs of the third little girl are hidden by long olive-green stockings. When they walk through a patch of sunlight between the shadows of the trees that are beginning to lengthen, the oblique rays play in their hair and surround their heads with a halo. From the side of the valley already engulfed in shadow there comes the faint tinkling of bells, which ceases and then begins again as invisible cows move from place to place. Above the foliage of the walnut trees, the sunlight sparkles on one of the galvanized metal strips of the church tower that have rusted to a soft red-gold color. The two funnymen are now standing right next to each other in the same ellipse where the beams from the four spotlights meet, green on its dark side, white on its light side, setting ablaze the giant sun embroidered in gold threads and spangles on the silk. The orchestra has stopped playing and the two clowns' loud, brassy voices rise in the silence, beneath the big top of the circus tent where, very high up in the semidarkness, one can see the chrome bars of the trapezes gleaming, cold and dangerous-looking, with their supports wrapped in red among the garlands of cords, cables, and rope ladders tied back along the poles. The white clown has cordially put one of his arms around the shoulders of his partner, who is listening attentively to what he is saying, nodding his head and voicing his agreement. From time to time a prolonged whinny or the roar of a wild animal can be heard outside. The dialogue consists of a series of questions and answers expressed in a rudimentary vocabulary, by means of which the new performer in the glittering costume sets up a series of verbal traps and misunderstandings based on facile puns and plays on words. Unlike the blood-colored mask frozen in an immutable expression of bewilderment and despair toward which it is leaning, the pale face with the thin lips has a repertory of pantomimed expressions, as limited as the vocabulary but sufficient to suggest, with the aid of sly winks in the direction of the audience, craftiness and cunning, patience mingled with vague disgust, stupefaction, or indignation. After a moment, doubtless as a result of the heat given off by the spotlights, cracks appear in the layer of white makeup that resembles plaster, splitting it open along the wrinkles in the clown's face, framing the mouth, or spreading out in little fans at the corners of the metallic eyes between the wrinkled, jade green, reptilian eyelids. The series of questions and answers follows the same pattern each time, in which the absence of anything unpredictable arouses the spectators' pleasure, inasmuch as they are capable of knowing in advance and foreseeing the expected denouement of each of the little sketches, marked by the inevitable slap with which the resplendent creature spitefully buffets his tatterdemalion partner. The sharp sound of the slap rings out like a pistol shot, giving rise to the same bursts of laughter from the audience each time. The clown whose face is bright red, as though from the effects of the slaps, turns away, howling with pain, his hand on his cheek, his back bent, turning round and round and lifting his knees high in the air, like someone suffering from a terrible toothache, as his tormentor, spreading his hands loaded with rings apart in a gesture of resignation, casts a sweeping circular glance around the entire audience, his eyes blinking, his lipless mouth cracking open in a broad smile that leaves a black hole visible in the moon-face, with a violet tongue, like that of a reptile, sticking out between gold eyeteeth. The boy who has been continually watching the spot where the motorcycle has disappeared, the barn, and the outskirts of the village suddenly nudges the other boy with his elbow, and the two of them look at the light patch formed in the distance by the mauve and white printed blouse which one can see on the other side of the hamlet now, making its way along a path leading up the north slope of the valley toward the woods. The path is lined with bushes, between which the mauve blouse appears and disappears. The bobs of the forgotten fishlines have drifted together, lying motionless on the water side by side, their long axes at right angles to the current, with fine silvery ripples spreading out in a V from them. The three little girls who are walking along the riverbank gradually draw closer. One of them is walking backward, facing the other two, moving one arm up and down, as though emphasizing certain parts of a story she is telling or beating out the rhythm of a counting-rhyme. Her legs are bare, and the checks of her pinafore are blue and white, exactly like the pinafore of one of the two little girls following her, her sister perhaps. The third one with the olive-green stockings is wearing a black schoolgirl's smock, brightened up by red edging. The mauve patch arrives at the point where the path leading upward, lined with hazelnut trees, reaches the edge of the woods and disappears. The rusty galvanized metal strip on the roof of the church steeple gleams even more brightly, like a gold fillet. The heads of the two boys are now turned in the same direction, scrutinizing the wooded slope, the edge of the coppice, and the barn. His attention entirely absorbed in keeping a sharp eye out, one of them is no longer remembering to hold his bamboo pole up, and the supple end of it dips in the water, now curving farther downward with the force of the current, now straightening again, moving jerkily backward and forward, raising a little aigrette of water each time. The shadow of the south slope reaches the opposite bank. Doubtless the woman has come out of the woods just behind the barn and has then walked along the side of it that is hidden, for the boys barely catch a glimpse of the mauve patch as it appears around the corner, rapidly walks along half the length of the front of the barn, and disappears behind the door that has been left ajar. The boys' eyes sparkle with excitement. They remain motionless for a moment longer, continuing to watch the barn where nothing is stirring now. Finally the bigger boy nudges the other one with his elbow again, and turning abruptly back toward the river, raises his fishing pole, pulling the tangled lines up with it. The two bobs lying side by side rise above the water, soon followed by the sinkers, and finally by the fishhooks with their worms still intact. Little droplets slide off the bobs, the sinkers, and the hooks, causing tiny silvery circles to form on the surface of the water, which are then carried away by the current. Swearing, the bigger of the two boys starts trying to disentangle the lines, suddenly says Wait, leaves the other boy to struggle with the fouled lines, and heads in the direction of the three little girls, who are very close now. They stop, raise their heads, and look at him as he says something to them and points to the little girl who is still sitting in the meadow, a few yards away from the riverbank. The white clown has again affectionately draped his arm around the shoulders of his partner, who stubbornly pulls away at first, and then gives in and stands there listening to him, shaking his head up and down like a donkey, as before, to show that he fully understands what the other clown is saying. The plaster white face is leaning to one side, the reptilian eyelids blinking rapidly across the diamantine eyes, the mouth slit open in the same sly smile, revealing the violet tongue. The other clown nods his head more and more energetically, lifts his frozen mask up into the beam from the spotlight, slaps his sides, crossing and uncrossing his arms, and shouts in his bizarre voice Oh it's e-e-e-e-asy! The three little girls nod their heads and two of them walk over to the little girl, each of them taking her by one hand. Followed by the third girl, they take a few running steps, raising the little girl up off the ground, whereupon she tucks her legs up under her and bursts out laughing, and then the two girls put her back down, raise her up again, and repeating this little game, proceed upstream along the river bank. The bigger of the two boys leans down, grabs the tangled fishlines out of the other boy's hand, makes an irritated gesture, wraps the two tangled lines around the poles any which way, sticks the fishhooks in a knot in them, stands up, looks all about, and with the other boy following him, crouches down and creeps along a hedge and then through a cornfield, in the direction of the barn. A cooler breath of air stirs the leaves of the poplars from time to time, turning them upward. For a moment all the leaves quiver, alternately revealing and hiding their silvery side, then fall back in place. The pale moon-shaped face draws closer, following an irregular path, appearing and disappearing between the black trunks, glistening with rain, of the trees in the stretch of park behind a brick building constructed in a pretentious hybrid style, decorated with bands of stone and flanked by fake turrets with pointed roofs. The ghastly pale mask follows a zigzag course, so to speak, shifting abruptly to one side and then to the other, at times falling flat on the ground, as though its possessor had tripped over a root or a bramble. The rain has stopped. Having finally reached the edge of the little wooded park, the face remains there, turned toward the façade with the unlighted windows, leaning against a tree trunk that half conceals a tuxedo jacket, the pleated front of a silk shirt with the collar unbuttoned, and one of the ends of a black bow tie hanging far down the shirt front, the other end being invisible. Despite the cold and the dampness, the shirt front is open to the waist, revealing the milky, hairless skin of the man's chest. Each time he exhales, little clouds of vapor escape from his half-open mouth, from the split lower lip of which there flows a light red trickle which his tongue keeps mechanically licking, cleaning from around the cut the blood which, lower down, on his chin, is beginning to coagulate. Another red trickle, mingled with mucus, is flowing down from one of his nostrils. The man wipes it away with the back of his hand, sniveling, and then wipes his hand on the side of his pants leg. By contrast with the watchful intensity of the gaze that remains fixed on the dark façade of the building, the movements of the tongue and the hand seem to take place beyond the control of the person's will and consciousness, as though he were unaware not only of the cold, but also of the cut on his lips and the gash across the bruised flesh over his cheekbone, or the swelling, already turned purple, that has half closed one of his eyes, whose gaze thus filters through no more than a thin slit. In addition to the traces of blood and mucus left by his hand each time he wipes it on his pants, they are also soiled by streaks of yellowish mud and splashes of vomit. Other mud stains are also visible on the elbows and along one side of the rainsoaked tuxedo with the shiny shoulders. A stretch of ground covered with gravel separates the edge of the park from the steps leading up to a terrace, in one corner of which are piled white enameled garden chairs and tables, which are not in use at this time of year. There are globes of frosted glass mounted on cast-iron pedestals at the four corners of the stone balustrade, but for the moment they are not lit, and the only illumination is that coming from a fifth globe above the door of the hotel leading to the terrace, in the center of the façade. Finally the moon-faced mask moves again, and stepping over the border of boxwood around the esplanade, the young man unsteadily makes his way toward the terrace. As he comes forward into the light, his wan face seems to grow paler still, at the same time taking on a greenish tinge which makes the trickles of dried blood on it appear almost black. Black trickles also stain the rumpled front of his shirt, the buttons of which have been torn off. The other end of the bow tie hangs out at his back, between the collar of his shirt and the collar of his tuxedo jacket, dangling down over the latter. Despite the precautions he is taking, the gravel crunches beneath the young man's feet, but no light appears in any of the windows. The diffuse light of the city illuminates the ceiling of low clouds drifting rapidly along above the network of crisscrossing black branches, the highest of which sway back and forth and bump together. From time to time the sound of a locomotive whistle or dull rumblings is carried on the wind. Once the shadow of the south slope has covered the barn, the half-shadow inside has grown darker and darker. Sitting up, her torso erect, her two legs pressed together and bent at the knee, the girl rearranges her rumpled hair, searching round about her on the old army overcoat for the hairpins with scalloped sides which she slips between her lips before taking them out one by one to pin down her straggling locks. Her movements reveal the tufts of hairs in her armpits stuck together with sweat, and her breasts sway slightly. The man with the curly hair is still lying on his back, his slightly parted legs stretched out, hampered by his blue cotton duck pants pulled down to his knees, forming accordion pleats above his black rubber boots streaked with grayish trickles of mud. His limp member is lying on its side, stretching across his groin and partway up the top of his thigh. His left arm idly circles the girl's waist and his hand mounts and descends along her side, caressing her hip, slipping one finger in the fold of her waist, then mounting again from time to time to her breast, the knuckles lightly touching its tip. Letting go of her hair, the girl's left hand descends, grasps the man's hand, and pushes it away from her body. The moment she lets go of it, however, it alights on her body once again, the girl pushing it away this time with a brusque gesture, and then, lowering her other arm and leaning on it, she shifts her buttocks, her head lowered now, searching around again on the army coat for the hairpins that have fallen out of her lips, protesting, still trying by means of little annoyed slaps to push away the hand, the back of which is now rubbing back and forth across the nipple of her right breast. In this new position, the entire weight of her body is resting on her right buttock and her right thigh lying flat on the floor, her two legs pressed together and bent to one side, the line of her spinal column forming a curve that begins at her lower back and rises almost vertically between her shoulder blades, the skin at her waist above her jutting hip forming three folds, and the bottom of her buttocks having turned a rosy pink beneath the weight of her body in the previous position. Against the body that glows luminously in the denser and denser shadow, the hand caressing it appears almost black. For a moment, taking advantage of the fact that the girl is busy fumbling about for her hairpins, the man brushes his hand back and forth across the curve of her breast more insistently, as though to test its elasticity, the supple flesh forming a slight hollow as the hand passes over it and then bounding back as the tip of the nipple gradually grows hard. As though possessed of a life of its own, the man's member lying across his groin begins to stir, animated by faint little quivers that cause it first to roll over the top of his thigh and then to swell and harden, gradually growing longer in a series of minute jerking motions. Encircled by the wrinkled crown of the foreskin, the pink tip of the glans appears, pierced with its little blind eye. Abandoning the breast, the hand brusquely buries itself between the girl's thighs pressed close together, attempting to thrust itself between them, fumbling about in the hairs, the girl giving a start and saying No, that's enough, drawing her buttocks back with an abrupt motion, rising up on her knees, stretching one arm out toward her clothes hanging on a part of the tractor that juts out, the man's two dark hands darting out and coming together around her hips at the same moment, the man's arms thrusting sideways with such a violent motion that it causes the girl to fall over on her side, the two bodies collapsing one on top of the other, the girl pushing the man's shoulders away with her outstretched arms, arching her back, the man's hands, taken by surprise by the suddenness of the motion, moving apart, letting go, the girl leaning on her extended right arm, bending her left leg back, then her right, then crouching on her knees with her buttocks thrust out, and finally standing up, the man's two hands, looking light-colored now against the black stockings, seizing her by the ankles and pulling her brutally off-balance, so that she topples over, as though mowed down by a scythe, on all fours on top of the torso of the man, who, taking advantage of her position, roughly pulls her knees apart and buries his head between her thighs, his rod, once again stiff and erect, now jutting out at an acute angle to his belly, with bluish veins snaking beneath the delicate skin of the sheath, the girl's protests dying away little by little, being gradually replaced by the sound of her breathing, growing faster and faster, her body inertly yielding, with only her haunches and her back swaying back and forth in faint undulations corresponding to the movements of the dark curly head of hair, like a ball between the phosphorescent thighs. The surface of the screen is separated lengthwise by a white, slightly curved band, dividing it into two unequal parts. The lower, narrower area is tinted that dark ocher, almost chestnut-brown, color that sawdust takes on when it has been wet down. In the upper part, which is in dark shadow, the torsos of the spectators, sitting crowded close together, are dimly outlined, their silhouettes distinguished from each other only by slightly varying intensities of black. The white band, at the base of which there can be seen the brown traces left by the hoofs of horses that have bumped against it from time to time, is bordered at the top by another, narrower band, of pomegranate-colored velvet, like the seat of a banquette. A bizarre creature is making its way along on all fours, in a simian posture, balancing on the velvet band. Its bare, inordinately long arms stand out in pink against the black background, illuminated by the spotlights which also highlight the white vest, the light gray pants, and the face tinged with green shadows, the flesh of which seems raw and bloody, its features crudely modeled in a soft paste, like a tragic rough study that has been abandoned, halfway between an animal and a man, bloated with vague puffy excrescences. From the sausage-shaped lips there emerge inarticulate cries, as though stifled by a gag placed over the mouth. The foreground of the right-hand side of the illustration is entirely occupied by the profile of a face completely covered with a layer of white grease paint and powder from which there stand out the eyelids coated with green makeup and the mouth with thin lips stretched into a smile that reveals a mauve-colored, batrachian tongue. Doubtless held by the invisible hand of the moon-white apparition, a leather leash runs up from the bottom of the picture and joins a collar placed around the neck of the half-simian, half-human creature which is balancing along the narrow crimson band. Awakened from his sleep by a series of knocks on the door, timid and discreet taps with a bent index finger first, then louder pounding with a fist, and finally furious kicks of a foot swinging violently against the wood, an old man in slippers, dressed in pants hastily slipped on over a woolen nightshirt, spies behind the glass panel of the door of the hotel the face of a drowned man, of a greenish-white color in the light of the globe outside, with dark stains running down from its nostrils and across its chin. A dialogue of deaf mutes is then carried on by the two persons through the glass, the features of the ghastly pale face contorted by a more and more intense fury, the arms gesticulating wildly, and then the face drawing back a few yards, the night porter thereupon catching a glimpse of the torn shirt front and the tuxedo, which also has stains on it, as the apparition takes a running jump forward and a tremendous kick causes the heavy oak door panel to reverberate and shake on its hinges, followed almost immediately by a second kick, the face having once again become impassive, the arms having ceased to gesticulate in any way, the person now being content merely to alternately draw back a few yards, take another running jump forward, give the door a tremendous kick, draw back, dash forward and lash out with his foot, draw back, and dash forward again, the pale mask devoid of all expression, like the face of a sleepwalker, until finally the night porter opens the door, prudently standing to one side, the drowned man in the tuxedo, propelled by his own momentum and off-balance, thereupon hurtling into the corridor, his torso horizontal, continuing on in great long strides for several yards, and finally managing to regain his balance at the end of his headlong dash and straighten up, turning around toward the night porter with unshaven cheeks and blinking eyelids, cutting the latter's protests short by shouting an insult at him before slumping over, clinging to the counter of the reception desk and leaning his torso across it to examine the board with the room keys hanging on it, and finally pointing at it with a shaky index finger, questioning the porter, and then, without waiting for an answer, shouting out one last insult and staggering up the stairs with steps covered with a pomegranate-colored runner. Standing in the center of the ring, the white clown is holding in his hand the end of a second leash leading to the neck of a little monkey also walking along on all fours on the velvet band in the same direction as the monkey-man on the opposite side of the ring. The two leashes run along the same axis, across the diameter of the ring, dividing it into two equal parts. The gilt bells attached to one of the two collars give merry tinkles accompanying the movements of the quadruped clown and the little monkey. In his right hand the white clown is holding the handle of a long whiplash with which he alternately flicks the monkey's buttocks and the outsize pants of the grotesque funnyman, clacking his tongue at the same time and offering brief cries of encouragement. The orchestra softly plays a melody with a skipping, staccato beat. Restrained laughter continues to be heard along the dark tiers of benches. The three little girls, only one of whom is now holding the hand of the smaller child, have reached a point not far from the waterfall whose continuous sibilant sound appears to have changed pitch, as though in the shadow that has now invaded the entire bottom of the valley sounds were being propagated in a different manner, as the sound of the sea, for instance, changes at night when the water becomes invisible and its pitch becomes lower and more solemn. A damp coolness full of the smell of growing things mounts from the meadows along the wooded slopes where the rocky cliffs that crown the southern side take on a gray, cold tinge, whereas those at the top of the opposite side are still touched by the sun's rays. One of the little girls is again walking backward, facing the other two, moving her arm rhythmically up and down in their direction, then brusquely slapping one of them on the shoulder and scampering off, her braids flying out behind her back, the other two girls starting to chase after her, the one holding the little girl by the hand and encouraging her to run too being soon outdistanced, whereupon she slows down, comes to a halt, and stands there next to the little girl whose wrist she is still clasping in her hand. After a moment she sits down in the grass and pulls the little girl down beside her, casting frequent glances in the direction in which the other two have disappeared. Finally she rises to her feet, calls to them several times, and receiving no answer, bends down toward the little girl, saying something to her and at the same time pointing insistently down at the very spot where the little girl is sitting, takes a few steps, returns to give her one last strict instruction, and then also scampers off. The little girl remains there all alone, her dress forming a clear patch against the solid green of the meadow. With clumsy gestures she arranges her bouquet, looks around her, leans over to one side to pick a flower, puts it with the ones she has already gathered, looks around her again, gets to her feet, and then, spying a clump of mauve flowers with long stems growing along the bank, goes down to the river. The water flows along rapidly with a silky, almost imperceptible sound, agitated by faint eddies along the edges or little whirlpools twisting round and round on its surface and then being carried swiftly off downstream by the current. One can make out clearly the yellowish tuff and the pebbles along the bottom, the largest of them covered in places by black moss. A trout, also black, swims diagonally across the current and disappears beneath the overhanging bank on the opposite side. Between the dark reflections of the leaves, little bits of sky gleam like pools of silver, undulating slightly. As he speeds up the clacking of his tongue and his repeated cries of encouragement, the white clown moves the handle of the whip in a series of sharp jerks, which are transmitted like a wave along the entire length of the lash, the end of which cracks with a sharp snapping sound, like a faint detonation. The little monkey quickens its pace, imitated by its human rival, who casts worried glances behind him, comically rolling his eyes in feigned terror. The rhythm of the piece being played by the band also speeds up. The level of laughter rises slightly. The girl has flopped forward, her head turned to one side between her arms, her cheek rubbing against the rough, dirty cloth of the army overcoat, her knees bent beneath her, her buttocks seemingly glued to the curly ball formed by the hair of the man lying stretched out underneath her in the opposite direction, his two hands tightly clutching the girl's light-colored hips. The black ball continues to move slightly. The girl begins to breathe faster and faster. Descending along her hips, the two dark hands slowly reach her buttocks, which they part, baring the cleft between them where the milky skin progressively takes on a sepia color as it spreads out in little folds forming a star around the anus, which all of a sudden the tip of the man's red, muscular tongue, looking almost black in the dark shadow, begins to lick, the film jamming in the projector at this precise moment and the two protagonists remaining suddenly frozen in this position, as though the life had suddenly drained out of them and time had stopped, the image that was only a passing phase, a simple transition, suddenly taking on a solemn, definitive dimension, as though the characters had been suddenly plastered against some invisible, transparent wall, trapped in the abruptly solidified air, being transformed between one moment and the next into inert objects, mere things among the things that surround them on the surface of the screen, which the eye, heretofore riveted on the moving forms, now gradually becomes aware of (the wrinkles in the old army overcoat, the chevron pattern standing out in relief on the enormous tire of the tractor above the couple, a brilliant reflection on the polished steel of the plowshares), until, as though to confirm the impression that a catastrophe has occurred, a blinding white spot appears, the flame-red edge of which rapidly grows larger and larger, indiscriminately devouring the two bodies locked in embrace, the farm implements, and the walls of the barn, the lights then coming on, and the screen blank now, a dull, uniform grayish color. Forming a pair with the slightly erotic engraving in which one can see the farm girl pushed backward into the hay by a farmhand, with two youngsters whose smiling faces are pressed against the gable window spying on them, is another engraving in the same style, entitled *The Enema*, showing a plump young woman lying stretched out on her belly on a rumpled bed, her legs spread apart, her back curving in, and her dimpled derrière thrust out toward a servant girl with an enormous syringe in her hand, the tip of which she is about to bury between the pink-tinted buttocks. Pulling back the folds of a drapery behind which he has perhaps slyly concealed himself, thanks to the venal complicity of the servant girl, a hand reveals the wanton face of a young man wearing a Louis XVI–style wig. The actress lying on her back, still in the same position, in the middle of the set representing a room in a luxury hotel, appears not to notice the two engravings, her wide-open eyes staring fixedly at the ceiling. The only change that has occurred in the position of the spread-eagled body (reminiscent of that of those lifeless bodies thrown out of a crashed car which have been half covered by a dirty blanket hastily drawn over them by the gendarmes) is that the left arm is dangling down one side, inert, the hand whose index finger had slid between the pages of the book now touching the carpet, onto which the book has fallen, so that its illustrated front cover is now visible. Other books and notebooks, all jumbled together, have been pushed back against the wall in an untidy pile, next to a marquetry-work writing desk with gilded bronze fittings. With the same suddenness which had frozen them motionless a few moments before, the two bodies begin to move on the screen that again gleams brightly at the far end of the room that has been plunged into darkness once more. It is several seconds before the spectators' eyes, still dazzled by the light, are able to identify the moving, faintly luminous forms in the deeper and deeper shadow of the barn. As a consequence of the splicing of the burned film, a certain number of frames have been skipped (or perhaps, through faulty synchronization, the lights in the room have not been turned off until a moment after the projection of the film has begun again), for the man is now on his knees behind the woman who is still lying face-down, arching her back so as to place her derrière at the height of the man's pelvis as it moves back and forth, slowly at times, but most often with a violence that causes his belly to slap against the smooth offered buttocks. Indistinct sounds, muffled by the thrusting motions, escape from the throat of the woman, whose cheek rubs against the rough cloth of the army coat with each stroke, so that one cannot understand her replies to the questions that the man asks her, in a voice at once savage, mocking, and triumphant, along with each of his most violent thrusts. Drawing her arms back, her torso then resting only on the top of her bosom and her shoulders, the woman clasps with her hands the posterior surface of the man's hairy thighs, which she presses against her, as though to make the rod penetrate her even more deeply. The man is leaning on the woman's haunches, his two arms outstretched, his torso vertical, his pants drooping in accordion pleats around the lower part of his thighs, baring his muscular buttocks which move back and forth more and more rapidly. Turned halfway round toward the circus ring, the band leader waves his baton in a more and more rapid beat. The two leashes held in the hand of the clown with the ghastly pale face standing square in the center of the piece of carpet and slowly pivoting around are now at right angles to each other and the distance between the little monkey and the simian figure that he is chasing diminishes. The spectators in the first row, who keep on laughing but instinctively draw back when the latter passes in front of them, can see the trickles of sweat running down from underneath the wig, leaving glistening trails in the white grease paint and the red makeup on his temples and cheeks. The droplets run together underneath his chin, where they quiver for a moment before falling off. Casting terrified glances behind him, the clown who is still on all fours and being closely pursued starts running now, waggling his rear end. Suddenly his suspenders give way and amid the even louder bursts of laughter, above which there can be heard the shrill squeals of women's voices, his baggy pants fall down in accordion pleats over his thighs, revealing a pair of cotton shorts and freeing a long tail, doubtless mounted on a spring, which unfolds above him in the shape of a question mark. The clown with the plaster-white face clacks his tongue even faster and cracks the lash of the whip in a series of sharp little detonations that mingle with the tinkling sounds of the bells on the two collars. The angle formed by the two leashes grows narrower and narrower. When the little monkey catches up with the man whose pants have fallen down, it jumps up on his back, and the man continues to gallop along, waggling his behind, until the white clown gives a violent tug on the leash which causes him to topple to one side and fall down inside the ring, where, amid the roars of laughter from the audience accompanied by repeated bangs on the big bass drum, he rolls about on the ground, emitting his bizarre and inarticulate cries, without managing to get rid of the little animal. It is now almost totally dark inside the barn, as well as almost totally silent, the only sound being the loud breathing of the couple, which gradually quiets down. One can barely make out the grayish form of the man's body, stretched out full length on top of the lighter-colored body of the girl, who is also lying stretched out full length on her belly. One of the two boys nudges the other with his elbow, and their cheeks on fire, the two of them move away from the barn, crawling backward through the grass to the clump of hazelnut trees where the bigger one grabs the two fish poles, and then, bent over double, runs through the meadow to the sunken path, into which the two of them leap, one after the other. A moment later they come out on the road leading to the sawmill and head toward the hamlet. The sun's rays are no longer striking the north slope of the valley. Vertical fringes, of a dark gray, almost black, color, like trails of ink leaking out of an overturned bottle, stretch across its surface. At the top of the south slope the rocks have taken on a bluish tinge. The clumps of vegetation above them are outlined in black against the absinthe-colored sky. In the frame of the window opening out on the night sky, not a breath of air now stirs the fronds of the palm trees, tinted an electric green by the floodlight situated below them, the tallest of them protruding slightly into the black rectangle. The woman is still lying in the same position. Someone (not the woman, for her left arm is still dangling down over the edge of the bed, her hand touching the carpet in the same place, alongside the illustrated cover of the novel) has changed the lighting, however, and the little bed lamp, the only one that is turned on, fills the room with a lilac-colored half-shadow. In the cone of harsh light beneath the lampshade, on the other hand, the naked shoulder and the dangling arm are sculpted, or rather, very sharply defined, and appear almost fleshless, the protruding areas, the hollows, the tendons, standing out underneath the skin in cruelly prominent relief. The cone of light also envelops the ashtray in which several cigarettes with greasy pink stains at one end are lying, crushed and twisted, as well as the package of cigarettes, the gold lighter, a glass half full of water, and a tube of pills. No sound of breaking surf can be heard echoing off the sea-wall promenade. The only sound is that coming up from the highway, the silky whoosh of tires of huge automobiles gliding slowly along the foot of the long cliff of façades, with rococo decorations or faced with marble, that follows the curve of the bay. From time to time, at more and more infrequent intervals as the night wears on, the rumble of a plane taking off or landing drowns out all the other noises, itself invisible, though its position lights, blinking alternately at the tip of the wings, can be seen gliding across the black rectangle of the window as it describes a sweeping curve upward or downward above the dark sea. The postcard showing the cliff lined with luxury hotels stretching out in a convex curve beneath a sky that is too bright a blue behind the clusters of cannas in the foreground is now leaning against one of the supports holding up the top of the sideboard. No one, on the other hand, seems to have touched the skinned rabbit, whose bloody head and paws with their little fur boots stick out from underneath the cloth with the pink edging, and the basket set down on the table appears not to have been touched either, still standing there full of fragrant yellow or violet-colored mushrooms with dirt-covered stems. It is night. The low-intensity bulb illuminating the kitchen projects on the oilcloth covering the table the black shadow of the head with the empty eye socket and those of the two motionless, parallel paws bent halfway back over the head in one final protesting gesture. The open door frames a black rectangle, at the base of which a diagonal line forms one edge of a triangle, inside which the light from the bulb illuminates the ground of the courtyard covered with gravel. The gravel crunches beneath the feet of persons who come in and go out in a succession of disorganized entrances and exits, speaking to each other in half-whispers, the crunching of the gravel ceasing when they step into the kitchen, the rope soles of a pair of women's cotton sandals making no sound on the stone floor, whereas a pair of men's high-top shoes resound loudly on it. In the intervals of silence one can hear the regular tick-tock of the pendulum of the clock and the stifled sobs of a woman, sitting on a chair in a recess next to the sideboard, her face hidden in the folds of an apron that she is pressing against her eyes. She is wearing black cotton sandals, black stockings, a brown skirt, and a mauve and white printed blouse. Seemingly blind and deaf to the commotion going on all about her, the old woman with the dog's head is sitting at the end of the table opposite the one where the rabbit is lying, with a large bowl in front of her, filled with a sort of dark yellow lumpy gruel, the consistency and smell of which are reminiscent of the food that one gives animals. Her black straw hat with the ragged edges is still tied around her head with the scarf, which is also black, with tiny gray flowerlets, knotted underneath her lower jaw like those chin straps that one puts on corpses. She looks like a wooden mannequin. Her gaze veiled by a sort of whitish cloud is directed immediately in front of her and slightly downward. Slowly, leaning her head over her bowl, she raises a tin spoon to her mouth, sipping in its contents with a sucking sound through puckered lips surrounded by wrinkles spreading out from them like a fan, as though the lips themselves were being sucked inside her toothless mouth, the flabby flesh of her cheeks bulging out as her gums masticate the gruel, dark lumps dribbling down her chin from time to time without her bothering to wipe them off. A tearful sound can also be heard now and again from the next room. From time to time one can hear, outside, one of the double doors of the iron gate creak as it opens. Several pocket flashlights with pale green, sky blue, or metallic red rectangular cases are lined up along one of the edges of the table. The gate opening onto the courtyard creaks again, and the younger of the two boys enters the kitchen, all out of breath. His eyes are red and he walks over to the table without looking at anyone, merely saying in a hoarse voice I've found one, and setting down next to the cases a new battery, the red and blue cardboard wrapping of which is decorated with a lion's head inside a circle. Neither the old woman, who continues to noisily suck up her thick soup, nor the young woman, whose shoulders are shaking with sobs and whose face is invisible behind her raised apron, says anything in reply. The boy then starts opening one of the cases and tries to insert the battery in it. His hands are trembling slightly. The decoration of the room, once stylishly ostentatious but now merely ponderously old-fashioned, the heavy drapes of pomegranate-colored velvet bordered with little round tufts, the ebony furniture upholstered in the same velvet material, the dark pink wallpaper decorated with bouquets in alternate rows make the entire room look dusty and stuffy. The radiator gives off a heavy heat, as though it too were full of dust. The young man with the badly swollen face lies across the bed whose mesh bedspread has not been removed. His body is completely naked except for his black socks, which are decorated with openwork clocks and which accentuate its almost feminine whiteness. In little piles of unequal size (first the black rain-soaked jacket of the tuxedo, then the elegant ruffled shirt, then the pants, the jockey shorts, and finally the muddy patent leather dress shoes removed without unlacing them), the garments, torn off rather than pulled off and simply thrown down on the floor one after the other, mark his path from the door to the bed, as though once the door had barely closed, the wearer of the garments had already begun ridding himself of them with the gestures of a sleepwalker, eventually finding himself standing naked next to the bed, onto which, pivoting around, he has collapsed face up, forgetting to take off his socks, and immediately fallen asleep. Making its way with great difficulty through his nostrils clogged with clots of blood, the air makes a gurgling sound with each of the intakes of breath that cause his hairless chest to rise. His head is thrown back, his mouth open, his eyes closed, one of his arms upraised and bent at the elbow, in the very position in which his body has landed when it fell suddenly back on the bed, the hand touching the curly pale blond hair, the other arm resting on the mesh bedspread in a gentle curve. The legs are slightly parted, the feet in the black socks dangling over the edge of the mattress, the long limp penis lying across the groin, the testicles hanging down in their sac of wrinkled skin which forms a sort of pleated drapery between the two balls below the root of the member. The sparseness of the curly hairs that form a yellowish tuft with the consistency of tow at the base of the belly but then thin out very soon, even before reaching the groin, reveals every detail of these vulnerable bodily parts. A bowl-shaped fixture of imitation jasper with green marblings, suspended from the ceiling by three little gilt chains, sheds a dim light throughout the room, the greater share of it being absorbed by the draperies, the dark furniture, the waxed wood floor, and the rug decorated with fruits, flowers, and leaves in colors turned gray by dust and time. On the velvet runner, also pomegranate-colored and bordered with little round tufts, covering the top of the table is a bouquet of orange blossoms with a little paper lace ruff around them, the stems of which, wrapped in silver paper, are tied with a large bow of tulle ribbon whose ends hang down over the edge of the table. A pair of white glazed kid gloves is lying alongside the bouquet. A brand-new suitcase, in yellow imitation leather, is standing alongside the wall near the door leading into the room. Another suitcase is lying flat on a folding wooden stand next to the wardrobe closet. A young woman dressed in a pearl-gray tailored suit is standing halfway between the table and an armchair turned to face the window, from which she has doubtless risen when the young man hurtled into the room. With a blank look in her eyes, she contemplates the milky naked body, the soft penis, the drooping testicle sac, the legs with the faint pale blond down, cut short at mid-calf by the black socks on which the traces of mud are beginning to dry. From time to time one can hear the whistle of a locomotive and the rumble of freight cars, muffled by the heavy drapes. Turning her eyes away from the naked body, the young woman takes a few aimless steps, and finally walks over to the window and pulls back one of the mesh curtains. From this side all that can be seen is a square that is absolutely deserted at this hour, with a raised concrete island in the middle, in the center of which is a tall arc lamp whose reflector casts a cold light on the paving stones, still wet with rain, and the streetcar tracks shining with a bluish gleam. The façade of the railroad station closing off the opposite side of the square is built in more or less the same architectural style as the hotel. It is made of bricks alternating with bands of stone, decorated in the center with a triangular pediment framing an illuminated clock. A glass marquee supported by slender iron pillars runs along the entire length of the second story, protecting the top of the flight of steps onto which five large doors with semicircular glass fanlights above them open out. Only the center door and one window on the second floor are lighted. The rain that has been falling all evening long has cleansed the air, and the buildings (the railway station, the shed with wooden walls painted a reddish earth color to the left of it, the outlying buildings) stand out in the most precise detail, the deserted setting being illuminated here and there, in addition to the center arc light, by symmetrically placed old-fashioned lampposts, each of them surrounded, as though by a flaring skirt, with its cone of light. There are no longer either woods, or a hamlet, or fields, or meadows: everything is indiscriminately engulfed in the opaque black of night, as though the darkness had settled in the bottom of the valley between the steep slopes on either side. It is only a very slight difference in the intensity of the blacks that allows one to barely distinguish the blurred shapes of the trees and bushes from the sky dotted here and there with a few faintly twinkling stars. The earth, the entire world seem to be covered over with a layer of thick, palpable ink, whose almost liquid contact one can feel on one's eyeballs, one's face, and even one's limbs. In the compacted shadows, the steady, continuous sibilant sound of the invisible waterfall bouncing off the invisible rock cliffs and the slopes of the valley seems itself like a sonorous concretion of silence, of a time without dimension. Powerful, unchanging, and omnipresent, it forms a sort of base for the strident chirring of the cicadas, also invisible, which weaves a kind of second sheet of silence, at an even, shrill pitch, with only the slightest modulations. From time to time, frightened by someone's approach, or to recover its strength, one of them, and then another, abruptly stops, whereupon it is succeeded (like a curtain opening on another curtain) by the same strident chirring, sounding fainter in the distance, but still continuous, repeated at intervals in the darkness, like a series of relays spaced at equal distances in all directions throughout the immensity of the vast darkness suddenly become vaster still. The little lights dancing here and there come and go, drawing closer together, then separating again, like fireflies, ridiculously small in the depth of the shadows, like the calls, the voices immediately drowned out by the monotonous dull roar of the waterfall and the deafening buzzing of the mating insects: the stubborn signals, tirelessly broadcast in the peaceful August night by hundreds of rigid legs frantically rubbing against cuirassed abdomens, ceaselessly appealing for blind, imperious, and ephemeral couplings. In the luminous cones of the flashlight beams searching along the banks, the leaves of the trees along the shores of the river, turned a harsh green color, cold and artificial, are outlined against the inky black background which immediately swallows them up again once they have been revealed for an instant, violently extirpated from the occult spell of the darkness in which one seems to perceive (on a lower, more secret note, and yet as powerful as the sound of the waterfall or that of the cicadas) a sort of vague palpitation, something as irrepressible as the mating calls: the mysterious palpitation of plant life (imperceptible movements of leaves, not because of the effect of some puff of air, but of slow unfoldings, slow twistings, as though they were opening, retracting, or closing at the mere contact, or rather the embrace, of the shadows), the imperious and ceaseless circulation of sap, the secret mutations of matter, the multiple breathing of the earth at night. Here and there a bough, a branch bending beneath its own weight, curves downward into the current which catches it up, releases it, and catches it up again in a continuous movement back and forth. The water flows along rapidly with a silky, barely audible rubbing sound, or else slows down, becoming almost stagnant in places, the beams of the flashlights swallowed up in a thick, creeping, dull green cloud. One can smell its icy odor, as though it were still carrying along the mineral breath of caverns, of rocks that are forever cold and dripping in the eternal darkness. From time to time a bird suddenly awakened from its sleep flies up out of a thicket amid a loud rustling of wings and leaves. Somewhere, from a stagnant branch of the river or some pond, there rises the discordant croaking of frogs. They too fall silent when footsteps approach, and one can then clearly hear the sounds their bodies make as they dive back into the water one after the other. Then one of them begins croaking again, a solemn, powerful, disproportionate call. Above the slope of the valley the sky gradually grows brighter and the moon appears. The rock cliffs on the top of the opposite slope suddenly emerge, pale white, from the darkness. The wind causing the cables stretched crisscross above the square to sway back and forth is still rapidly driving across the sky the low clouds illuminated by the reflections of the street lamps on the paving stones that are beginning to dry. In the space between the railway station and the shed, one can see the freight cars of a train that has stopped, two of them with solid sides painted, like the shed, a reddish earth color, and a platform car whose load is covered with a greenish-gray canvas. A railway worker walks along the train, swinging his lantern that projects its dancing yellowish light on the sides of the cars. The moon appears, disappears, reappears in a rift in the scudding clouds, almost full, unusually white. Its hard light projects on the paving stones the sharply outlined shadows of the façade of the railway station, of the shed, of the bare branches of a tree half-hidden by a building on the left. The suffused light from the lampposts attenuates the opacity of the shadows they cast, which remain transparent, not black like those out in the country. The big hand of the clock with the illuminated dial in the pediment on the front of the railway station jumps abruptly from one number to the next, and falls motionless once again. Shortly thereafter one hears the prolonged creaking of the wheels of a streetcar rounding a curve and the motor unit followed by its train of cars soon makes its appearance, coming from the left, slows down, and stops in front of the railway station. The uprights of the windows and the upper part of the streetcar are painted yellow, and the solid part below a dull brown decorated with yellow stripes. Along the roofs of the cars are narrow sheet-metal panels with advertisements painted on them: BROADWAY DEPARTMENT STORE—THE CITY'S NEWEST, in black letters against a yellow background, framed by the words LATEST FASHIONS—FOR MEN AND WOMEN, in smaller capitals, and at the top of the cars the name of a brand of whiskey traced in a spiky cursive script in white against a red background. Projected by the moonlight, the weave of the mesh curtains, drawn to one side by the woman's hand, is repeated, in a distorted dark gray pattern, on her pearl-gray tailored suit. The first streetcar with the motor unit and the cars trailing along behind it is crowded with dark silhouettes hurrying toward the exits, all of them heading for the railway station where, almost at the same moment, a train comes in, blowing its whistle, and halts amid the strident screech of its brakes. Three of the huge doors beneath the marquee are now lighted up. Shortly thereafter other dark silhouettes stream out of the center door, the only one open, slightly jostling those entering, and quickly head for the stopped streetcar, some of them at a run. The majority of them are carrying canvas satchels or bulging briefcases. One can hear the puffs of steam regularly emitted by the halted locomotive, the smoke rising in the moonlight above the roof of the shed in a black cloud, colored yellow at its base by the light from one of the lampposts along the platform. The moon disappears. The dark silhouettes crowd into the front car of the streetcar and those trailing behind. The last ones to arrive remain standing between the benches, one arm uplifted toward the straps hanging from the ceiling. The young woman lets the curtain fall back and turns toward the bed from which there continue to come snores intermingled with gurgling noises. Finally she walks over to the bed, and bending down, lifts up the legs dangling over the edge and tries to raise them onto the bed. During this entire operation, her eyes avoid the testicles and the limp penis that has rolled over onto the thigh. When the naked body is stretched out full length on the bed, she tugs at the torso so as to bring it toward her and make room for herself on the other side, and then somehow manages to pull the fringed bedspread partway over the naked body. At no time has the sleeping man awakened. Only the rhythm of the gurgles has changed, though again becoming regular almost immediately thereafter. After casting one last glance at the naked body on the bed, the young woman walks back over to the window and again draws the curtain aside. The square is now deserted. One can hear the panting sound of the locomotive gradually growing fainter as it moves off in the distance, and see the lighted windows of the passenger cars gliding along more and more rapidly between the main building of the station and the shed, until the last car disappears on the left, revealing the motionless freight train. The young woman walks away from the window, and standing in front of a large mirror hanging on the wall, with the gestures of a sleepwalker, slowly takes off the jacket and skirt of her tailored suit, and then her blouse which she hangs up on a hanger in the wardrobe. Then she sits down on the edge of an armchair, and after having slipped off her shoes, removes her stockings which she carefully drapes over the back of the chair before sitting down again, clad only in her brassiere and a silk half-slip, edged in lace and wrinkled at the waist. She sits there for a moment, staring into space, listening to the irregular gurgling sound coming from the other end of the room. Finally she gets up, walks over and closes the velvet drapes with a brusque movement, goes over to the mirror, and taking off her brassiere, contemplates her naked breasts. The mirror is surrounded by a gilded molding with rounded corners and decorated with a row of beads that are also gilded. Her rather large, slightly sagging breasts, have pale pink areolas and very small, rough, sepia-colored nipples. The waistband of her half-slip compresses the flesh at her waist, which forms a faint roll of fat above it. By contrast with the white silk half-slip, her skin seems amber-colored. Her eyes not leaving her image in the mirror, the young woman removes her slip and panties and then stands there, stark naked, her feet together, in front of the mirror. Her frizzy hair is a yellow-brown color, her bulging eyes with dark brown pupils protruding beneath the eyebrows plucked in too perfect an arch stare fixedly, like glass eyes, at her naked body with somewhat soft contours, the belly that curves outward, the broad thighs, the knees and the naked feet tinged a rosy pink. In the center of the body the hairy tuft of the pubis, of a darker brown than the hair on the head, spreads out over a wide area, like a parasitical growth or a sort of prominent wig stuck onto the smooth flesh. The two oblique sides of the triangle do not coincide, however, with the folds of the groin, the path of which the eye can follow, the thick hairs forming instead a sort of wide bar at the bottom of the belly and becoming sparser as they descend to form a narrow point lower down, which seems to plunge between the clearly visible lips of the vulva, with skin tinged gray rather than sepia, around which the hairs spread out like a short beard divided by a part down the middle. From outside, through the heavy velvet drapes, sounds filter in at closer intervals now: a factory whistle, the creaking of the wheels of a streetcar rounding a curve once again, then the balky motor of a truck or a bus which refuses to start but finally begins to turn over evenly, though at a high rate of speed, its rumble causing the windowpanes to shake. One of the sleeping man's hands clumsily clutches at the bedspread several times and finally he manages to pull it off his body and throw it back, without waking up, however, and then the labored snoring begins again. In the background the pale horizontal form of his body intersects, at a right angle, the reflection, likewise pale, of the young woman standing in front of the mirror, rubbing the fingers of her hand back and forth over the frizzy, shadowy fleece of her pubis with a robot-like gesture. From her pointed nose above the mouth with lips that are too thin and smeared with lipstick, her big bulging eyes do not even appear to see the long mold of flesh like a wax statue standing in front of her, or the hand which, abandoning the pubis, mounts along the body, passes over the belly, the navel, as the other hand also rises, both simultaneously reaching the level of the breasts, around which they cup themselves and lift them up. Outside, the big motor roars several times as the driver presses down repeatedly on the throttle, and finally the car—or the truck —takes off in a paroxysm of vibrations that shake the windowpanes so hard they almost break, then little by little the racket dies down. The heavy breasts swell and bulge out slightly over the tops of the cupped hands. Their pale nipples swell and jut forward. The protruding eyes continue to stare blankly. The moonlight bathes the countryside in a pale, uniform light, like a silvery coat of paint pierced by the completely black shadows of the trees, the bushes, and the hedges. The rock cliffs are a chalky white color, separated from the dark blue sky in which there is no longer a single star shining by the dark line of trees at the top of them. One can again see the configuration of the valley now, its steep wooded slopes, and the long, pale rectangle of the wall of the steeple crowned with its pyramid of dark tiles, one of the metal strips along its edge shining with a cold gleam. One can also see glistening patches on the surface of the river bordered on each side by the black masses of the bushes. Little by little, as the moon rises, a wispy fog seems to rise at the same time, spreading out from the river in a thin, faintly wavy layer, hovering just above the ground and the grass turned gray with dew, and then shredding apart, revealing here and there, like the islands of an archipelago, the dark masses of the trees. In the beams from the little pocket flashlights, the light fog becomes tinged with yellow and more opaque. The dew weighs down the bottoms of the pants of those walking along the riverbank, and black fringes of moisture mount upward from them. The bowls of little dancing lights now spread out for a distance of about five hundred yards on either side of the river, outlining its meandering course. The sound of the waterfall, though still a steady sibilant roar, seems to have changed pitch once again, however, as though, after the light has appeared, it were propagating itself more freely, through lighter air, passing from one octave to another. A dog barks somewhere, and one can also hear the cry of a nighthawk echoing in the woods. Suddenly a voice calls out, and all the little lights strung out along the two banks of the river move along rapidly in short little jerks and gather around one of the lights, which bobs up and down at first, and then ceases to move. For some time now no plane has taken off or turned to make a landing on the runway of the airport at the other end of the bay, the parking area of which, planted with yuccas, palm trees, and oleanders, must now be deserted. The floodlights hidden among the beds of cannas have been turned off and the fronds of the palm tree whose top projects above the lower edge of the window are now illuminated only by the fainter lights of the lampposts and the lobby of the hotel. The traffic on the highway has also thinned out considerably and the silky sound of the tires rubbing against the asphalt as they slowly roll along has given way to a relative silence, disturbed only now and again by the roar of a sports car rushing by at top speed, which rapidly grows fainter and fainter. The camera slowly moves in on the woman still lying stretched out on the bed in the same position, who seems to glide toward the spectator, head first, as though being borne along on a moving conveyor belt, until her rumpled hair, her upturned face with open, staring eyes fill the entire screen, the camera then pivoting slightly to the left as it continues to move forward with no change of focus, the eye, the cheek, the lips which now occupy the right-hand side of the screen becoming blurred as the contours and the details of the breast, its nipple, and the shoulder in the cone of light from the little lamp become more distinct, and then the head and the breast disappearing, the camera now moving along the bare arm down to the hand whose fingers lightly touch the carpet alongside the illustrated cover of the book, which finally occupies the entire top of the screen. The title of the novel stands out in red letters on a white band at the bottom of the cover illustration, above which the name of the author is printed in green letters, against a background of bare black crisscrossing branches standing out against a very dark gray sky that grows lighter and lighter as one's eye moves downward toward a salmon-colored rift in the dark clouds, just above the horizon. Two men stand silhouetted, like characters in a Chinese shadow play, against this opening, at the edge of a woods. The body of one of them is arching backward, the knees flexed, the head thrown back, the chin pointing toward the sky, one arm bent upward as though to ward off blows, and the other already hanging down toward the ground, onto which he will soon collapse, while his adversary, with one arm curving out in front of him, the fist upraised, is immobilized in that position in which, for a fraction of a second, a body remains frozen after having arrived at the limit of its impetus once it has delivered a violent uppercut. To the right, approximately halfway up the cover, is a long wall of dark red bricks, drawn in perspective, against which, depicted in larger scale and in more precise detail than the silhouettes of the two men fighting, two persons, a man and a woman, are standing locked in an embrace, the latter with her back to the wall. Above the top of this wall one can make out factory chimneys spewing out black smoke which eventually touches the ceiling of clouds at the top of the cover illustration. In the foreground and to the left is the face of a young woman wearing a bridal veil. Her eyes brimming with tears, her knit eyebrows, the outline of her half-open mouth express despair. The axis of her face is inclined at an angle of approximately fifty-five degrees. At the very bottom of the lower corner, one of her hands is shown, pressing the tulle veil against her breast. Immediately next to the woman's face, and looking at it with an annoyed and guilty expression, is that of a young man with curly blond hair atop a sheeplike head, framed in sideburns of a yellowish tow color. There is no continuity between the various parts of the illustration. The two men at the edge of the woods with the black branches and the tree trunks, the long brick wall against which the couple locked in embrace are leaning, and the two faces in the foreground occupying the greater part of the rectangle constitute three different compositions separated by fuzzy areas, as though they were being simultaneously projected by three machines onto the screen of smoke and black clouds. The figures in the middle distance (the man and the woman locked in embrace) and those, farther away, of the two men fighting, are bathed, however, in the very same atmosphere of rain, cold, and dampness, revealed by the wet reflections on the trunks of the trees and the paving stones of the blind alleyway at the foot of the wall. The two boys under the apple tree are now lying stretched out in the grass. One of them, his arms crossed under the nape of his neck, chewing on the stem of an umbel, his left leg bent halfway back, his knee high in the air, is swinging the foot of his other leg, crossed over the first one, back and forth. The second boy is lying on his side, turned toward his companion, his left elbow bent back, his left hand supporting his head, his right hand toying with the bits of film lined up on the grass between their two bodies, picking up one of them from time to time and holding it up to the sky to look through it, though in an absent-minded way, as though he were thinking of something else. Still chewing on the stem and merely shifting it to one corner of his mouth, the bigger boy says I know where he screws her. The other boy turns his eyes away from the image he has been looking at and says Oh you do, do you?! Continuing to swing his foot back and forth, the bigger boy says In the Martins' barn, near the woods, the one with the circus poster on it. The other boy says How do you know? Smiling complacently, the bigger boy says How much do you want to bet me? The smaller one says again How do you know? The first one says Will you keep your mouth shut about it? The other one says Who do you take me for anyway how do you know? The first one says How much do you want to bet me? The smaller one says again How do you know? The first one says I saw them he works for them he's got the keys. The other one says No kidding? The first one says No kidding. The other one says You saw them? The bigger boy says I sure did I even looked inside there's a hole. The smaller one says You saw them? The bigger one says Man you should see the size of the cock on him, geez it's really something! The other boy says Who? The bigger one says The wop you dummy who do you think? He uncrosses his arms, clenches one hand into a fist, and hits the crook of his elbow with his other hand, causing the fist to rise. Like that! The other boy says Oh yeah? The bigger one crosses his arms behind the nape of his neck again and begins swinging his foot back and forth once more. He says Will you keep your mouth shut about it? The other one says again Who do you take me for anyway No kidding? The bigger one says again Will you keep your mouth shut? The other one says Listen have I . . . The bigger one says Have you got another butt on you Will you promise not to say a word? The smaller one fumbles around in his pocket and says Listen, damn it, have I ever . . . The bigger one carefully smooths the wrinkles out of the crumpled cigarette and straightens it out, lights it in the flame of the match that the other boy holds out to him, casts a wary glance all about them, fanning away the puff of smoke he has exhaled and says You have to be careful not to have a run-in with those wops they're rough characters he fucks her bare-ass naked. The smaller one says Bare-ass naked? His cheeks turn a flaming red. The other boy says Man you ought to see the cock on him With a great big tip that's all red when he takes it out! The smaller boy lays the little strip of film that he has been absent-mindedly holding in his fingers down on the grass, at the tail end of the others. From this angle, that is to say when the light is no longer shining through it, the little images grow dark. One can barely discern the black silhouette of the fat man standing with his feet together, his head turned to one side as though he were trying to make out what is happening behind the door whose handle he is holding in one of his hands, at the end of his forearm that juts out horizontally from the dark mass of his body. He changes his mind, however, lets go of the wrought-bronze handle, and with his bent index finger taps on the door several times, softly at first, and then a bit louder. No reply being forthcoming, his hand returns to the door handle, turning it cautiously, and the door opens a crack. Leaning slightly forward and bringing his eye closer, he spies first in the narrow vertical slit the book thrown down on the carpet, the dangling hand, and then, as his glance sweeps upward, the arm, the bare breast rising and falling in the rhythm of slow, regular breathing, and finally the upturned face and the eyelids that are now closed. It seems to him, however, that he can see them quiver slightly, like those of someone deliberately keeping them closed and pretending to be asleep. He stands there motionless for a moment, apparently hesitating, and then, with the same cautious gesture, gently closes the door. He continues to stand there in the same place for a few moments longer, his right arm dangling down his side, his left hand resting on his lower back once again, in the same familiar gesture of weariness, his left elbow forming behind his body an angle with a rounded apex, his face a motionless pinkish violet patch, standing out sharply in the light and etched with dark hollow shadows. Finally he turns halfway

around, and crossing the carpet that muffles the sound of his
heavy footfalls, he goes back over to the divan and sinks down on
it. On the low Chinese-style table with the curved, decorated legs
and the long black lacquer top, at one end of which are a local
paper and the *Financial Times,* folded back to the page with the
stock market quotations, one of those enormous jigsaw puzzles
that Anglo-Saxons are so fond of, measuring approximately
twenty by thirty inches, is laid out. The puzzle is almost completely put together. Some twenty small pieces, with sinuous
contours, are spread out in a disorderly array to the right of it.
The man sits there for a moment, contemplating the puzzle without moving, and then he leans forward and his hand picks up one
of the little pieces, holding it above the nearly completed puzzle
for a few seconds as he rapidly glances over it before finding the
right place for the piece and inserting it. The large puzzle shows a
hamlet of twenty houses or so, situated in a valley hemmed in by
wooded slopes topped with cliffs of rock. A river lined with
trees and bushes snakes back and forth across meadows and
fields of corn or wheat. The meadows run up along the slopes to
the edges of woods consisting of dense thickets of ash trees,
hornbeam elms, beeches, or hazelnut trees. The roofs of the
house and the barns form purplish-brown geometric patches amid
the green of the foliage. Their sharp outer edges are protected
by strips of galvanized metal, turned yellow with rust, certain of
which gleam in the sun. At the far left of the picture, one can see
in the distance, alongside a large building, a flour mill doubtless,
or a sawmill, the white trace of a waterfall amid the clumps of
vegetation surrounding it and hiding the foot of it. Between the
waterfall and the hamlet the river bends in two curves in opposite
directions, forming an S, the second bend skirting the first houses
of the hamlet before running through it, cutting it approximately
in two, and spanned by a stone bridge. Before the bridge, upstream from it, stands the church, the steeple of which is clearly
visible: a simple tower, square in section, made of gray stone,
rising above a clump of walnut trees with green leaves that have

a slight yellow tinge, its roof consisting of a squat pyramid of brown tiles, the outer edges of which are also protected by galvanized metal strips. Vegetable gardens and plum orchards stretch out around the village and behind the houses to the edge of the river, some of them planted with a few ornamental shrubs, elderberries with large fat flowers of a yellowish off-white, or lilac bushes. The surface of the river ripples and sparkles in the places where it runs across a shallow bottom. Elsewhere it reflects like a polished mirror the vegetation along the banks and the steep wooded slope of the valley, which a light fog has turned a bluish color. In the backyard of one of the houses, a man is busy splitting logs. The steel blade of the axe gleams when he swings it upward. Two boys with their fish poles propped up alongside them are lying on their bellies across the parapet of the bridge, just above the first arch, their heads almost touching, attentively scrutinizing the river bottom, toward which one of them is pointing his outstretched index finger. Just beyond the bridge the ground on one side of the road slopes down to the water's edge, gradually taking on a dark brownish tinge as it becomes damp, marked with innumerable hollow imprints of the hoofs of animals coming down to the river to drink, and dotted with greenish cow-pies among the clods of dirt. Two cows with beige hides spotted with white patches, their front legs buried in the water up to the knees, are drinking from the river. Another one alongside them has already emerged from the water, with trickles of slaver that shine in the sun hanging down from its mouth. A fourth cow is climbing back up the slope, using its neck as a counterweight to keep its balance, as a fifth one steps onto the bridge, heading in the direction of the church. A youngster with stiff tow-colored hair chopped off in a ragged line across the back of his neck and wearing men's huge high-top shoes without laces hurries the two cows still lingering at the river's edge along with his stick. The smooth-surfaced millrace passes underneath the first arch of the bridge. Its overflow runs down over a low wall, perpendicular to the middle piling of the bridge, forming a little cascade, the water then flowing rapidly again, glistening in the sun, between steep banks on which clumps of water willows and enormous bluish green leaves shaped like little ruffled collars or flaring funnels are growing. Leaning forward, his thighs parted, his left forearm resting on his left thigh, the man with the powerful but heavy build sets the last little piece in place with his right hand, and the last little island of black lacquer disappears, filled in with a part of the hair of one of the boys, standing out against the polished, dark olive-colored surface of the river. The man then sits there motionless, the arm that has set the piece in place now resting, like the other one, on the corresponding thigh, his two hands hanging down between his spread knees. His red face, bent forward, is completely bathed in a violet-colored half-tone with black shadows here and there, as though it had been roughly filled in by a painter who had abandoned his work after having laid down a few hasty preliminary brush strokes. Only the top of the forehead and the hair are in full light. Between the sound of cars driving quickly by, at more and more infrequent intervals now, one can hear, spaced out in the silence, like shivers so to speak: a silky, rustling sound running along the shore and the faint sound of the surf flowing in across the pebbles. The usherettes have already put their coats on and are pulling back the drapes across the exit doors, with a metallic sound of curtain rings gliding along brass rods. Sensing that the performance is nearly over, a few spectators are beginning to rise to their feet here and there in the auditorium, and a number of seats slap against the seat backs as they spring upright. These sharp sounds are multiplied as they echo off the bare walls of the enormous half-empty movie theater. The man gradually raises his head and turns it slowly around, the black shadows on his face drawing back and gliding away as he does so, and then he arrests its movement, looking over his shoulder through his half-closed eyelids in the direction of the bedroom, from which no sound emerges. The usherettes slide wedge-shaped stops under the doors to hold them open. Through one of the doors one can see the wet paving stones of the street and the brick front of the house facing the movie theater. With the same slow movement, the man's head returns to its initial position. He sits there motionless for a few seconds, then suddenly his right hand violently sweeps back and forth across the surface of the table, breaking up the puzzle and scattering the little pieces all about. Their meandering edges have been deliberately cut in such a way that none of them, viewed individually, shows the entire image of a person, an animal, or even a face. With very rare exceptions (the ocher of the cows' hides, the gray of the stones of the bridge, the violet-brown of the roofs), they range along the entire scale of greens (emerald, Nile green, apple green, jade, moss green, olive), and constitute a sort of archipelago of tiny islands, curving in to form bays and gulfs and curving out to form capes and promontories, against the red background of the carpet. The seat bottoms are now slapping against the seat backs all over the auditorium, in a deafening chorus, and the house lights go on. Blinking their eyes, a bit dazzled and confused, like someone just awakening from a sound sleep, the spectators put on their coats, wind scarves and mufflers around their necks, and crowd into the side aisles separating the rows of empty seats, forming several lines that slowly move toward the exits. The rain outside has stopped, and the wind is making the light bulbs suspended at intervals above the long artery sway back and forth. One can hear the doors of a number of cars slam shut as they take off one after the other. Finally only one car, the door handles of which are decorated with bows of rain-soaked tulle, remains parked against the opposite curb, a little farther up the street from the movie theater whose outside lights go out as the usherettes draw the iron grille and the last spectators walk off in little groups, the collars of their coats turned up, hunching over in the wind, along the sidewalks that soon are deserted.